GODDESS'S CHOICE

THE CHILDREN OF THE GODS ORIGINS
BOOK 1

I. T. LUCAS

THE CHILDREN OF THE GODS ORIGINS

Annani's Story

1: Goddess's Choice

Areana's Story

2: Goddess's Hope

THE CHILDREN OF THE GODS

Kian & Syssi's story

1: Dark Stranger The Dream

2: Dark Stranger Revealed

3: Dark Stranger Immortal

Dark Stranger Trilogy + Goddess's Choice—part 1

Amanda's story

4: Dark Enemy Taken

5: Dark Enemy Captive

6: Dark Enemy Redeemed

Kri & Michael's Story

6.5: My Dark Amazon Novella

Andrew's Story

7: Dark Warrior Mine

8: Dark Warrior's Promise

9: Dark Warrior's Destiny

10: Dark Warrior's Legacy

Bhathian & Eva's Story

11: Dark Guardian Found

12: Dark Guardian Craved

13: Dark Guardian's Mate

Brundar & Calypso's Story

14: Dark Angel's Obsession

15: Dark Angel's Seduction

16: Dark Angel's Surrender

Turner's Story

17: Dark Operative: A Shadow of Death

18: Dark Operative: A Glimmer of Hope

19: Dark Operative: The Dawn of Love

Anandur's Story

20: Dark Survivor Awakened

21: Dark Survivor Echoes of Love

22: Dark Survivor Reunited

Magnus & Vivian's Story

23: Dark Widow's Secret

FOR A FREE NARRATION OF

Goddess's Choice

JOIN THE VIP CLUB AT ITLUCAS.COM

Available only on the VIP Portal at itlucas.com:

FREE Audiobook, Preview chapters, And other goodies offered only to my VIPs.

TRY THE SERIES ON

AUDIBLE

CONTENTS

PART 1

PART 2

PART 3

PART 4

PART 1

FIRST KISS

PRELUDE

First kiss.

If done right, it left an impression to last a lifetime, or in Annani's case, millennia. Five thousand years, give or take a few hundred.

Age was meaningless to a goddess.

But even after all these years, and all that Annani had witnessed, the fire that first kiss had ignited at the tender age of seventeen still burned hot in her heart.

After all, it was the most important kiss of all times, affecting the destiny of gods, immortals, and humans, and altering the course of history.

1

ANNANI

Five thousand years ago, give or take a few centuries.

"Are you ready, my lady?"

"Patience, Gulan. I need a moment." With deft fingers, Annani attached a small silk sack to her spun-gold belt. After tying the belt around her waist, she tugged on her makeshift carrier to ensure it was safe enough for her uncle's lapis lazuli tablet. Satisfied with the bag's structural integrity, she carefully inserted the tablet inside it and then rearranged the folds of her dress to conceal it.

The device was priceless and irreplaceable, not because it was the only one of its kind, but because of the information it contained.

Ekin had once told her that what was stored inside his tablet could fill several human libraries, and as far as she knew, her uncle did not keep a copy. So unless Ekin had all that information stored in his head, the thing was indeed priceless and irreplaceable.

And yet, he let her borrow it whenever she pleased.

Sometimes Annani did not even ask, taking it without his permission. Ekin did not mind. The scientist was an easygoing god, not a stickler for the rules like her father—the head god, the commander, the one everybody had to obey, or else.

Except, even though Annani had broken the rules plenty of times, she did not know what that 'or else' meant. Her father's idea of punishment was a stern look and an admonishment not to do it again.

It was not very scary, nor was it an effective deterrent to further mischief.

Her maid paled. "My lady, you cannot bring the tablet to the throne room."

Twisting her hands, the girl looked at the folds of Annani's dress, which were not doing much to hide the carrier and the square tablet inside it. Every time she moved, the thing bumped against her thigh and the folds parted to reveal it.

"I will hold the fabric over the sack. No one is going to notice a thing."

With her beauty and her attitude, the guards and whoever else roamed the palace corridors were not going to pay attention to her dress. They would be too focused on their future ruler's face.

Her maid emitted a soft resigned sigh.

Poor Gulan. The girl was a year older and more than a foot taller than Annani, not to mention stronger than most men—even immortals—but she had the heart of a little rabbit.

And to think Annani's parents entrusted her safety to Gulan's hands.

Her impressive size did not make the girl brave, and even though she was loyal to a fault and loved Annani as much as Annani loved her back, it was doubtful Gulan would be any good against any actual attackers. The girl did not have the heart of a warrior. She was timid and shy, and instead of taking pride in her size and incredible strength, she was embarrassed about it.

No matter. Gulan was her best friend, and she would not have traded her for anyone else in the world. Besides, Annani was not worried about a traitorous attack.

The people loved her—gods, immortals, and humans alike—she was everyone's favorite. As one of the few pure-blooded gods born to her people and the leading couple's only daughter, she was precious beyond compare and cherished by all.

No one harbored ill intentions towards her.

Annani patted Gulan's arm. "You worry too much. Watching my father and mother and their endless meetings with immortal and human pompous dignitaries bores me to no end. I need the tablet to keep me occupied. Imagine how embarrassed they would be if I yawned or fell asleep in the middle of an important audience. I might even snore." She winked.

Gulan could not help a small smile. "You do not snore, my lady."

"Yes, I do, and you know it."

Gulan opened the door, peering outside as if there was danger lurking in the palace's corridors that she needed to look out for.

It was comical.

First of all, because Gulan would sooner faint than

fight, and secondly, because the two guards posted outside Annani's room were more than capable of taking care of any threat to her.

"Good afternoon, my lady." The two bowed.

She nodded, looking down her nose at them. "To you as well. May the Fates smile upon you with kindness." The official greeting was a big fat clue that she was not happy with them.

The traitors.

Her haughty attitude had not gone unnoticed. Shamed, the guards trailed silently behind her and Gulan with their heads hung low. Feeling a little sorry for them, even though they did not deserve her pity, Annani glanced back. "Who won the game last night? Was it you, Gumer?"

"Yes, my lady."

"And why was I not invited?"

Gumer blushed. "We thought you were asleep and did not wish to disturb you."

Liar.

She shook her head. "Admit the truth, Gumer. You did not want me there because I always win."

Annani was the undefeated champion of the five-stone gambling game, but that was no reason to exclude her. After all, she never took the winnings for herself, distributing the coins between the guards instead.

"It is true that you always win, my lady. But that was not the reason. It was your head tutor's threat to report us to your father."

Ugh, she was going to have that grouchy old goat dismissed.

The nightly game with the guards was one of the few

bright spots in her uneventful court life. That mean man had no right to threaten anyone in her entourage.

Besides, she had no need for the dumb tutor. Her uncle's tablet contained all the knowledge Annani could ever seek, and when the subject was too difficult for her to comprehend, Ekin was more than happy to explain.

Her uncle was the smartest of the gods.

Not that Annani would ever dare such an utterance in front of her father. The half-brothers were not on the best of terms. Ahn thought of Ekin as an irresponsible philanderer, which was true, and Ekin thought of Ahn as a stick-in-the-mud, which was also true.

"I will ask my father's permission to participate."

Badum groaned. "You are going to get us in trouble, my lady."

She waved a hand. "You worry too much. My father grants all of my wishes." Except excusing her from the mandatory daily attendance in the throne room.

It was an unimaginable torture reserved only for the children of those in power. The successors. And to think people thought her lucky. As if she, or any other seventeen-year-old, wanted this mantle of responsibility instead of having fun.

But her parents wished to prepare Annani for her role as the future ruler of the realm—a complete waste of time in her opinion. There was plenty of time to learn all about court politics when she was much older and actually cared about all that yawn-inducing stuff.

Unless catastrophe struck, it would be thousands of years before Ahn and Nai stepped down and Annani had to ascend to the throne.

Gulan put a finger to her lips, signaling the guards to

keep quiet, and opened the back door to the throne room. The entry was hidden from those conferring within by a perforated partition, which allowed Annani to sneak in and out unnoticed.

In one of her cleverer maneuvers, she had asked to be allowed to sit back there with Gulan, hidden from the visiting dignitaries as she supposedly listened in on their dealings. Annani had convinced her parents that more could be learned by observing people unseen from behind the partition. Her best argument had been that if she were less concerned with appearing regal and dignified, she could pay better attention.

Her parents had accepted the excuse and even praised her for coming up with the idea.

Sitting with Gulan behind the partition made the whole thing infinitely more bearable. Using finger gestures, which they had developed over the years into a whole language, allowed them to gossip with no one any the wiser. It also meant that as long as she kept the green glow from the tablet at the lowest setting, Annani could read instead of listening to the proceedings she had absolutely no interest in.

Today, though, turned out to be different.

She was in for a big surprise.

Even before taking her seat, Annani heard a voice she would recognize anywhere.

Khiann?

What is he doing here?

As Gulan started forming words with her fingers, Annani waved a hand to stop her.

Peeking through one of the holes in the partition, she felt her knees turn into goo at the sight of him. She had not seen Khiann up close since he had graduated school over two years ago, and the only other time was during a celebratory ball she had been forced to spend up on the dais with her parents.

He had disappointed her greatly that day, and she had cried herself to sleep later that night.

Annani remembered every detail from that ball vividly. She had waited with bated breath for Khiann to approach the dais with his parents, hoping he would smile at her, eager for him to see how much she had grown since the last time he had seen her and notice that she was no longer a little girl, but was turning into a young woman.

Instead, he had bowed respectfully without sparing her a glance and then departed to mingle with the rest of the guests.

Khiann had acted as if he did not know that she existed, which was preposterous since she was Annani—the most important young goddess of the realm.

But that had happened a year ago, and a lot had changed since.

Khiann was no longer a boy. He was a grown man, and there was no way he could ignore her now. A year ago she was still considered a girl and forbidden to him, but now she was of age and permissible. Not to mention that she was considered the most beautiful, most coveted goddess of them all.

Annani was also free to choose a lover.

Well, not exactly.

It would have been true if she were anyone other than Annani, the next ruler of the realm. Unlike other immortal females her age, and young goddesses if there were any, she was already promised to a god, and therefore deemed taken. But she had no intention of ever mating with the god her father had made the ill-conceived pact with.

Ahn should have asked her before promising her hand to Mortdh. Unfortunately for her, he had done the deed when Annani was still a baby. If it were up to her, she would have never chosen Mortdh as her intended.

She would have chosen Khiann.

He was exactly the kind of mate Annani dreamed of —a young, honorable god, who had a sense of humor and was gorgeous like a god should be.

It was not that Mortdh's visage was unseemly, he was as beautiful as any other god, but his godly beauty must have been marred by his cruel nature because all she could see was his ugliness.

How did her father fail to see the darkness inside that male?

How could he have promised his daughter, who he claimed to love more than anything in the world, to a man like Mortdh?

It was all about politics.

Mortdh was powerful, the only god who posed a threat to her parents' rule. By giving him Annani, her father hoped to keep Mortdh's ambitions at bay until Ahn and Nai decided to step down.

The ambitious god would get his wish then.

The thing was, her father's plan had one glaring flaw that even she, a seventeen-year-old goddess, saw as clearly as if it had been already written in the historical records. It might have postponed the eventuality of Mortdh's rule, but the result would be the same.

With the wrong male on the throne, the gods' way of life would change for the worse, and with them that of everyone else, immortals and humans alike.

Still, even if she was wrong about Mortdh, and he turned out to be a decent ruler, love should have been more important than political alliances—her father's love for her to start with, and then her love for her future mate, and his for her.

Mortdh, who had many immortal concubines and dozens of children, cared nothing for Annani. He had not bothered to come see her even once.

She could have settled for a mate that was not her truelove, but not an indifferent one who saw her only as a means to an end.

With a sigh and a deep longing in her heart, Annani looked at Khiann.

If only he had shown the slightest interest in her, she could have entertained the illusion of him being the one fate had intended for her.

2

KHIANN

"Greetings, my lord." Khiann's father bowed low. "May I present my son and business partner, Khiann."

Dipping his head even lower than his father, Khiann managed to deliver the words he had rehearsed before coming in a surprisingly steady voice. "It is a great honor to be allowed an audience, my lord." He watched with horror as a single drop of sweat detached from his forehead, landing on the stone floor with a loud plop.

Ahn pretended not to notice. "Welcome, please be seated." The ruler waved a magnanimous hand at the two chairs below his dais.

"It is a pleasure to see you all grown up, Khiann, and helping your father in his endeavors," Nai said in her melodious voice. "Navohn must be very proud of you."

He bowed again. "Thank you, my lady."

Why in damnation was he sweating so profusely?

It was not hot in the throne room, nor was it humid. As with all of the gods' abodes, the walls were made from thick stone and there were no windows to admit the outside heat or the glaring sun. Nevertheless, his breathing felt stifled.

It was all in his head. There was no shortage of air and it was not stagnant. The diagonal shafts that were carved into the stone provided adequate air circulation, cooling it as it passed through cubits of rock before entering the great hall.

Imagining the air flow helped him breathe easier, but his brain was still not functioning properly—the words exchanged between Ahn and his father not coalescing into anything coherent.

He had spent hours preparing for his first official meeting with the leader of the gods as his father's business partner, rehearsing everything from his words of greeting to how deep he was going to bow, but apparently, all that preparation had done little to calm his shaky nerves.

If it were up to him, Khiann would have waited a few more years, but his father, who was inordinately proud of his achievements, had insisted that it was time for him to meet their leaders in his official capacity, and not only as Navohn and Yaeni's son.

Ever since Khiann had finished his schooling he had been apprenticed to his father, the only god who'd turned to commerce and left politics and the governing of humans and immortals to the other gods.

Did Ahn approve of his father's decision?

Or did the ruler share the disparaging opinion of the other gods in regards to Navohn's chosen occupation?

Upon reflection, that was the main reason for Khiann's nervousness. He would have a hard time controlling his temper if Ahn's attitude toward his father was as disrespectful as that of some of the other gods.

The move that had made their family rich beyond measure had at the same time lowered their status in the eyes of their peers. Commerce was held in higher regard than manufacturing, and manufacturing was held in higher regard than farming, but all three were considered occupations unbecoming of gods.

The gods were not supposed to do work of any kind. They were supposed to rule.

Except for the few who served as Ahn's assistants, the other gods were each in charge of one of the city-states. Those in committed relationships split their time between the neighboring cities they each ruled.

Their seemingly parasitic way of life didn't bother Khiann. In exchange for the goods and the free labor and the worship they were getting, the gods provided leadership and guidance to the humans and immortals they were in charge of, ensuring peace between the city-states.

Without their leadership, the humans, and perhaps even the immortals, would have instigated endless wars over territories and resources.

Humans were a violent species, prone to irrational behavior. The gods were essential for their social stability and their prosperity.

Not that the gods had always been peaceful. Khiann's father had told him some of their people's history, and it had not been pretty. Maybe that was the reason for omitting it from the school curriculum. The gods of this new generation were taught that they were a benevolent people, seeking only to improve the lives of others.

Sometimes Khiann wished his father had not told him the truth. He had been much happier believing in the moral superiority of his people. His only hope was that they had evolved, leaving their bloody past behind them for good and committing to the utopia they had created in their new home.

The question was how long it would last.

Fortunately, gods lived very long lives, which meant their history was measured in tens of thousands of years, as opposed to mere centuries for humans.

"I am heading out east in eleven days, my lord," Khiann's father said. "The journey should take about seventeen days and the trade two or three. I should be back in about forty-eight days." He clapped Khiann's back. "My son is in charge while I am gone, and he can take care of supplying the local goods."

Ahn regarded Khiann with a smile. "How are you enjoying working for your father?"

Khiann bowed. "I enjoy it very much, my lord. I find commerce exhilarating." If Ahn harbored hopes that Khiann was vying for a leadership position in a new city-state, he was going to be disappointed.

The human population was proliferating, and the new generation of pure-blooded gods numbered only twenty-three members, with each expected to take leadership of a new city-state at some point. But Khiann wanted nothing of the sort. He wanted to travel, to take caravans to distant lands and encounter new people, then bring back goods no one had ever seen before, and stories no one had ever heard before.

Tedium and boredom were the bane of the gods' never-ending existence. Khiann saw himself as the deliverer of the antidote to that malady. At least for himself. Staying cooped up in a temple built in his honor and living off human offerings was not his idea of a good life.

Ahn sighed. "Ah, to be so young and free. To travel, to see the world. I understand your fascination with trade. But one day you may wish to do something more meaningful."

Was that a barb intended to belittle his father's choice?

Hiding his grimace, Khiann bowed again, sitting down as soon as Ahn returned his attention to Navohn.

As the two droned on about this and that, he glanced around the throne room, admiring the various artifacts displayed on pedestals or hanging on the walls, many of which had been gifts from his father that he had brought from his travels.

Apparently, Ahn put a high value on them. Or was it Nai's work?

The goddess did not talk much, but on the rare occasion that she did, everyone listened because every word counted. Despite her humble origins, Nai was smart, stately, and refined, just as one would expect from the ruler's mate.

It was a mystery how those two created a child like Annani—the little hellion.

A smile lifted his lips as he was reminded of her. On the days they had had school together, he used to watch her, her antics and theatrics a source of endless entertainment.

Naturally, he had kept his fascination with the princess a secret, pretending he wasn't paying attention. Hopefully, that was the impression that he had left. To even think of her was disrespectful of her status, not to mention that it was grossly inappropriate to have indecent thoughts about someone so young.

Annani was pure fire. Red flaming hair, eyes blazing with intelligence and mischief, and a giant personality to match. A powerhouse contained in a tiny yet stunning package.

She was hailed as the most beautiful goddess of them all, and it was the honest truth, but her beauty was so much more than skin deep.

Shining like the sun, cheerful, confident, but never condescending, and always into one prank or another but none malicious.

The girl was all heart.

No wonder every human, immortal, and god was in love with her.

Khiann had been taken by her even when she was a young girl, but he had done his best to avoid her in school. It was wrong for a thirteen-year-old boy in the grips of puberty to even notice an innocent eleven-year-old girl.

His infatuation had only deepened as he had watched her grow and blossom. At the same time, though, he had done some growing up himself and had realized the sad truth that Annani was an impossible dream.

The princess could never be his. Even if she were not promised to Mortdh, the second most powerful god after Ahn, Khiann would have never been considered a suitable match for her. Not by Annani nor her parents.

Her mate would one day rule by her side, and as a merchant's son, Khiann was neither qualified nor suitable for the position.

3

ANNANI

I am moving up front, Annani signed with her fingers, then untied the belt holding the sack with her tablet and handed it to Gulan.

Taking the thing with trembling hands, Gulan held it to her chest and crossed her arms over the treasure. The girl hated it when Annani forced her to become an accomplice in her many little transgressions, like holding on to a priceless tablet that should have never left Ekin's study. But that was exactly why Annani wanted Gulan to hold on to it. The thing was safer in her arms than on the chair or the floor where one of the guards could accidentally step on it.

Leaving the protection of the partition, Annani slid into her designated chair behind her mother. Nai glanced back and nodded her approval, mistakenly assuming that Annani was finally showing real interest in court proceedings.

Annani nodded back and smiled, waiting for her mother to turn away before daring to take a peek at

Khiann. She had not seen him in so long. Had he changed much? Had his shoulders become even wider?

Fates, she had spent so many nights fantasizing about Khiann that she was almost afraid the reality of him would disappoint.

Not that it was likely. Khiann had been such a handsome boy, and the last time she had seen him he had taken her breath away. At nineteen, he was a fully grown man and probably so gorgeous and manly that it would be painful to look at him and not be able to touch him.

The thought of the many females, immortal and human, that he must have bedded by now made her irrationally jealous whenever it flitted through her head. Unlike her, Khiann was free to do as he pleased. He was not her intended, or anyone else's, and even if he were, he would not have been expected to remain chaste like a human maiden.

Gods lived by different rules.

Except for Annani, who was promised before reaching the age of consent and therefore had no chance of fooling around before joining her intended, which in her case was not going to happen anytime soon, nor did she want it to. Mortdh was in no hurry to mate her. After all, her ascent to the throne was thousands of years into the future, and until then, he had no interest in her.

It was so unfair. She had needs like any other goddess of age, but the only way she could slake them was with her own hand while thinking about a certain handsome young god. The same one who was still pretending not to notice her, same as he had done in school.

With one big difference.

Since the last time the two of them had interacted, Annani had learned to see past people's pretenses.

The throne room was saturated with the scent of burning incense, a precaution all gods and immortals employed when entertaining guests to mask the scent of their emotions from others of their kind.

Scenting Khiann's reaction to her was not possible.

But after years of sitting behind the partition and observing people who were trying to hide this or that, Annani had learned to decipher the subtler cues. Like Khiann's breathing becoming more labored, or the rigid set of his incredible shoulders that had indeed grown wider since the last time she had seen him.

He was not indifferent to her. Maybe he had never been.

Interesting.

Further testing was needed.

Tilting her body sideways to peer at him from behind her mother's back, Annani lowered her eyes and smiled coyly.

As his eyes shot to her for a brief moment, Khiann's breath hitched, but he quickly averted his gaze and returned his focus to Ahn.

Annani frowned. His reaction or lack thereof was bordering on rude. He had not acknowledged her presence with even the slightest of nods.

Why was he acting this way?

She was of age. He was allowed to look as much as he wanted. It was not an offense. As a god, he even had the right to ask her father's permission to court her. After all, she was not mated yet, and a woman was allowed to change her mind, even when she was promised to someone.

He obviously found her desirable, and he could no longer think of her as too young. Was it because she was promised to another?

It still was not an offense to try and win her heart. Their law stated that any woman, even a lowly human, was free to choose her mate—her wishes superseding any and all prior promises and agreements made on her behalf.

That was why most engagements were kept short.

As long as she and vile Mortdh were not married, she could choose someone else, and no one could do a thing about it. At least in theory. In real life, familial and economic considerations often dictated paths that were not paved with love.

Most matings among gods were prearranged, and only a handful were true-love matches—rare and coveted pairings the Fates bestowed upon the few lucky ones.

Perhaps Khiann was hers?

Annani did not know him well enough to claim to love him, but she desired him and was quite certain that he desired her back. It was a start, and she wanted a chance to find out if there was more.

Even a tiny chance of finding her true-love match was worth pursuing, and justified taking big risks.

Annani smiled again even though Khiann was not looking. Perhaps he could feel her smile and turn toward her. But he did not. Sitting all rigid and tensed, his shoulders so tight his muscles must have hurt, Khiann did not let his gaze veer away from Ahn for a moment.

Perhaps they were discussing something really important? She listened for a few minutes.

"Your in-house armed escort is not enough this time, Navohn. There are rumors of increased activity by the bandit tribes along the trade routes. I am willing to fortify your caravan's security with additional force."

"It would be much appreciated, my lord. I will gladly pay for the service."

"A discount on the palace supplies would suffice."

"You are most generous, my lord."

Boring.

They were not discussing anything that required Khiann's full attention. Bandits attacking caravans was not news to anyone.

Then again, as a merchant's son, Khiann probably traveled with the caravans.

Suddenly, all that talk about extra protection on the way gained utmost importance to her.

The thought of Khiann getting attacked by bandits sent a shudder down Annani's spine.

She should talk with her father and have him double the escort he was offering Navohn. A god was not as invincible as they had the human population believe. A sword could sever a god's head just as easily as a human's.

It was wrong of Navohn to drag his son along on his acquisition expeditions. Instead of exposing Khiann to the dangers of the road, he should have insisted that his son be assigned the leadership of a city-state, and that he spend his days safe behind the walls of his temple like most other gods, worshiped and adored by the humans under his rule.

And just like that the final piece of the puzzle that was Khiann fell into place.

There could have been another reason for his refusal to acknowledge her. As a merchant, he might have considered himself unworthy of her.

Fates, how she hated politics.

Khiann was a god, and it did not matter what his or his father's occupation was. Not to her. And if it mattered to her parents, she would let them know exactly what she thought of their snobbery.

Her father kept reiterating how important it was not to judge people by their status or financial standing, but to pay attention to their intelligence and integrity instead. Ahn could not contradict his own words without losing her respect.

But as long as Khiann refused to even look at her, all of that was irrelevant.

Discreetly, Annani moved her chair sideways, so she was no longer hidden behind her mother, and crossed her legs, letting her dress ride up a little and show her shapely calves.

When that did not help, she changed positions again, hoping the rustle of fabric would attract Khiann's attention.

This time he could not help himself and cast her a quick glance, which she caught and held onto.

Transfixed, Khiann's eyes remained trapped in her hold, and a moment later they started to glow.

Yes!

He was attracted to her. A male's eyes could not lie. The glow betrayed what he had been so desperately trying to hide.

The problem was that they were not alone, and her parents might notice his response.

Annani smiled her most charming smile and lifted two fingers to her eyes, signaling him to lower his.

He caught her meaning immediately and dipped his head, pretending to brush specks of dust from his tunic.

Smart man, but a stubborn one.

Khiann would never take the first step no matter how many signals and interested looks she cast his way. As her mother liked to say, males were too obtuse to interpret signals and needed to be told in plain language what to do.

It was up to her to initiate the first contact.

Not a problem. Annani was very good at taking charge. She was not the type of woman who waited for others to advance her agenda or who prayed to the Fates to grant her wishes.

Well, she did that too, but not without doing everything in her power to help providence along.

4

KHIANN

"You did well in there, son," Khiann's father said as they left the palace grounds.

"I do not know why you would think so. I said very little." Khiann had been surprised to find his voice at all, and even more so when it had come out sounding confident. Ahn was an intimidating god on any given day, and doubly so when a young god was having his first audience with the ruler of the realm and it was crucial for him to leave a good impression.

Still, the official introduction had gone well, and he had managed getting his nerves under control. Until Annani had showed up, destroying his tenuous equilibrium. The young goddess was so stunningly beautiful that no man could take his eyes off her without using every last bit of his willpower to do so.

She was an impossible to ignore distraction that had set Khiann's heart aflutter and had tied his gut in knots. And to make matters even worse, Annani had flirted with him, taunting him with her coy smiles and meaningful glances as if they were alone in the throne room and not in the company of her parents, the rulers of the realm.

Spoiled princess.

Her intention had not been malicious. She was a young girl who had just recently come of age and was probably trying out her feminine wiles on every male at court, oblivious to the fact that she was jeopardizing Khiann's first and most important audience with her parents.

His father clapped his back. "You sounded confident and answered Ahn's questions eloquently. That in itself is no small achievement for a young god like yourself. I could tell Ahn was impressed."

"I doubt that. I might have sounded confident, but I am sure Ahn scented my nervousness despite the amount of incense burning in that room."

"I did not smell anything, and I was sitting right next to you. But even if he had, this was exactly the way you should have felt. Ahn would have been suspicious if you showed no fear at all. He would have thought you reckless or even disrespectful."

It would have been beneficial to have this piece of advice before the audience. The experience would have been a lot less stressful.

"I am glad I was not a disappointment to you, Father."

"Never. Now, go on and unwind. You deserve it after all this excitement."

Khiann bowed. "Thank you, Father."

He watched as everyone other than his squire

departed, Navohn and his assistant riding in the carriage, their armed escort following on horseback.

His father was a cautious man, never leaving the house without several bodyguards at his side, not even when going to an official meeting in the palace. On second thought, though, he might have done it more for the sake of appearances than safety concerns. It was a show of wealth.

"So, how exactly do you want to unwind?" his squire asked.

"A bucket of beer would do."

Esag grinned. "Are you going to share?"

"No, I am going to finish it all by myself," he said, watching Esag's grin turn into a frown.

Khiann let his friend stew for a few moments before taking pity on the idiot. "I am going to get one for me and one for you. Surviving an audience with Ahn calls for a celebration."

The grin was back. "You are most gracious, my lord." Esag bowed his head in mock deference.

They had been friends for too long to bother with formalities. Esag had been serving as Khiann's squire for years, and right from the start he had become his best friend and confidant. Unless they had company who expected a servant to behave like one, Esag could say and do whatever he felt in the mood for.

"Oh, so now that I am buying you beer I am suddenly 'my lord'?"

"Yes, your highness, or should I say, your hardness?" Esag winked.

"Fates, was I that obvious? Did anyone notice?"

"I did, and maybe the flirtatious tiny princess did as

well, but the others did not see a thing. No one was staring at your crotch."

Khiann exhaled a relieved breath. "Thank the merciful Fates."

"She wants you."

Khiann waved a dismissive hand. "Annani is young and beautiful and probably flirts with everyone in court. Besides, she is promised to Mortdh."

Shaking his head, Esag took Khiann by the elbow and led him away from the main route. Once they reached a secluded area, he glanced around to ensure they were alone and far away from prying ears. "I know it is not my place to talk ill of a god, but Mortdh is not a good male. The princess deserves someone better."

Khiann cocked a brow. "Like me?"

"Why not? She obviously likes you. If I were in her tiny shoes, I would do everything in my power to escape an eternity of misery. Think about it. Her only chance of changing her future is to find a new suitor and declare him as her chosen."

Thinking of sweet Annani in the clutches of that cruel god felt like shards of stone were tearing his heart apart, but contrary to Esag's naive assumptions, there was nothing Khiann could do to help her.

"Political matings are not about love. Ahn seeks to keep the realm unified. A promise of future leadership as Annani's mate is the only thing that keeps Mortdh from attempting to seize it by force now."

"I do not know much about politics and I care even less. I just feel sorry for the princess."

Indeed. With Mortdh as her mate, the shining bright star of their people might dim or even flicker out of existence. It was a dark future Khiann did not wish to contemplate. His only consolation was that it would be thousands of years before Ahn and Nai stepped down in favor of Annani. Many things could happen between now and then, and some calamity could befall Mortdh, freeing the princess.

But that was in the hands of the Fates, and they did not always do the right thing.

When they reached Ninkasi's temple, servants rushed to provide a table for them, which was not easy since the place was full. But he had nothing to worry about. Every server in the tavern knew that Navohn's son left generous tips.

He and Esag were seated in no time.

As Khiann observed the many patrons eagerly spending their gold in the tavern, he had to applaud the enterprising goddess's cleverness. By referring to her chain of taverns as temples to worship her invention of beer, she had managed to sidestep the whole stigma attached to commerce.

Not that there was anything shameful about it. Trade was considered a respectable occupation for humans and immortals, just not for gods. Gods were supposed to be above all material pursuits, which was ridiculous since they all lived in decadent luxury provided by their worshipers.

"Two pails of beer, please," Khiann ordered.

"Yes, my lord." Ninkasi's servant bowed deep.

Esag straddled the stool and leaned his elbows on the wooden table. "Imagine how you would have felt if your father promised you to some ugly hag."

"All goddesses are beautiful."

Esag quirked a brow. "Other than you know who, there are no other unmated goddesses currently available. So you either settle for a divorced one seeking a young male, or a lowly immortal. The third option is to wait for one to come of age or be born."

As if he did not know that. "I do not mind mating a nice immortal girl." It was a lie; not the part about minding an immortal as opposed to a pureblooded goddess, but the one about mating with anyone other than Annani.

Perhaps he would just remain unmated. That would be best. He could have as many immortal and human lovers as he pleased without committing to a female he did not love.

Esag sighed. "I should not talk. My family promised me to Ashegan when I was five."

"What is wrong with Ashegan? She is a beautiful immortal."

"Yes, but she is not the one I want. She is so vacuous that I cannot carry a conversation with her about anything other than gossip."

Ashegan's family was wealthy. To secure her hand for Esag was a boon for his family and a chance of better matings for his two sisters. Immortal matings were as much about politics and securing alliances as godly ones.

"If you were free to choose, who would it be?" Khiann asked.

"I do not have anyone I am interested in. But the princess's maid caught my eye."

Khiann chuckled. That was surprising. Out of all the girls Esag could have found attractive, Annani's statuesque maid would not have been Khiann's first guess, or the hundredth. "Gulan? She is huge!"

Esag looked offended on her behalf. "She is tall, not huge. And that is a lot of woman to love." He waggled his brows.

"She can also pick you up and toss you across the yard. I have seen her do that."

The girl was freakishly strong, which was why she had been chosen as Annani's companion—another layer of security to keep the mischievous goddess from getting in trouble.

As if anyone could accomplish that.

Annani was uncontrollable, and whoever thought otherwise either did not know her or was a fool. Not that he would ever dare call her father that. But parents were often blind when it came to their children. Ahn probably had no idea about half of the stunts his daughter had pulled. If he had, he would have never allowed her to leave her rooms without a cadre of bodyguards.

5

ANNANI

"You are going to be the death of me, my lady." Gulan's hand twisting was becoming frantic.

At this rate, she was going to rub the skin off her fingers.

"Nonsense. You are immortal." A third-generation, but still not someone who should fear death. Gulan's mother was the immortal daughter of immortal parents, but her father was a human.

Very unfortunate for her and her family.

Hopefully, Gulan and her little sister Tula would secure good immortal mates. They would need to support their mother after their father died. Not that he was such a great provider, but the mother was even less so, lacking any money-making skills whatsoever.

Gulan was saving every coin she earned as Annani's maid and companion in case her family became dependent on her.

"I do not like involving Tula in your schemes, my lady. She is too young for the whip."

Annani rolled her eyes. "You worry too much. No one is going to whip Tula or you. If I get caught, I will take the blame and say that I forced you two to obey me. With my reputation, no one is going to question that."

Gulan sighed. "Why do you need Tula, though? I can lie in your bed and pretend to be you while you are gone."

Annani put her hands on her hips. "Really? You are more than a head taller than I am. No one will believe it is me in the bed. And if I borrow your clothes, I will drown in them. Tula is just my size." She pointed at the girl sitting on her bed.

"She is twelve."

Annani grimaced. "I know. I do not need reminders about my diminutive size."

"What I meant was that she is just a child."

"No, I am not." Tula spoke up for the first time, crossing her arms over her chest. "I already have my cycle, which makes me a woman."

Gulan bent at the waist to bring her face level with her sister's. "You are a little girl who does not even have breasts yet. A human might be considered a woman at twelve, but you are not a human. You are an immortal, which means you are considered a child until your seventeenth birthday."

Tula pouted and jutted her chin out. "I am half human."

"There is no such a thing. You are either immortal or human. You cannot be half of each."

Annani waved a hand between the sisters. "If you girls are done arguing, I need Tula to undress."

Gulan bowed. "Yes, my lady."

After years of friendship and countless arguments, the girl still could not call Annani by her given name, not even when there was no one around.

Tula went behind the dressing screen and removed her tunic, draping it over the top of it. "I am ready, my lady."

"Gulan, give your sister one of my dresses."

"Yes, my lady."

Clad in each other's clothes, Annani and Tula examined their reflections in the mirror and sighed in unison.

"I need to cover my hair," Annani said. Her flaming red tresses were too distinct and unusual. Only gods and some of the immortals had hair that color and none in her exact shade. The commoner garb would not do much as far as hiding her identity as long as all that hair was visible.

"Me too," Tula said.

Gulan handed them both long prayer scarves. "That is the best I could do."

It was a human custom to cover the head with a scarf when visiting the gods' temples for worship. Very few of the immortals adopted the custom, and naturally none of the gods.

Thinking, Annani tapped a finger on her lips.

Her immortal guards could be easily thralled as she left the room, and she could then use the side corridors reserved for servants to exit the palace. Sneaking out was not going to be a problem. Outside the palace walls, she would pretend to be just another human female on her way to a temple.

The problem was Tula and her black hair. No one went to sleep with a prayer shawl, and Annani's red mane was unmistakable.

A drying cloth, though, could work.

"Gulan, fill up a tub with water, and get Tula a drying cloth to wrap around her head as if her hair is wet."

Tula giggled. "That will fool them."

"Hopefully, it will not be needed. If anyone knocks on the door, ignore them. They will assume I am sleeping."

Right then a knock sounded, and both Tula and Annani rushed to hide behind the screen.

Gulan opened the door. "Thank you." She took the flowers Annani had asked her guards for.

To converse freely with her coconspirators, she needed to either get rid of the guards or cast a silencing shroud over her room. The problem with a shroud was that the guards would have felt it and gotten suspicious.

Sending them on an errand was better.

A little thrall had convinced them that it was okay to abandon their post. Nothing harmful, of course. Annani had been very careful to use as little as possible. After all, she cared for her guards dearly and was loath to inflict damage on their minds, which frequent thralls were known to cause.

Fortunately, immortals could not thrall each other, just humans, and gods could thrall both immortals and humans but not each other. That limited the playing field somewhat.

Now that the guards were back, they needed to switch to either hand gestures or low whispers.

Once the tub was full, Annani used her fingers to communicate. *Make some splashing noises,* she told her maid.

The girl nodded and dipped her hand in the water, moving it back and forth.

"Oh, I just love taking baths," Annani said out loud while wrapping the drying cloth around Tula's hair.

"Get in bed," she whispered to the girl.

Next, Annani braided her long hair, wrapped it several times around her head, and then covered it all with the shawl, pinning it in place with hairpins.

She waited a few more minutes and then yawned audibly. "I am so tired. The bath was so relaxing that all I want to do now is take a nap."

"Yes, my lady," Gulan said.

"You and your sister can go. I do not need you while I am resting. Come back in two hours and bring me those sweet cakes I love from the market."

"Yes, my lady."

"And if you please, also tell the guards not to let anyone disturb me until you are back. I need my beauty sleep."

"Yes, my lady."

With Gulan's arm wrapped around her shoulders, Annani did not even need to thrall the guards on her way out, which made her feel a little less guilty about her deception. The guards were her friends, but unlike Gulan whose loyalty was first and foremost to Annani, the guards' loyalty was to Annani's father.

Letting them in on her scheme would have gotten

them in real trouble with him, the least of which would have been a whipping. Her father would have ordered them to be whipped first and then dismissed them from service, leaving their families without a source of income.

"Do you know the way to Khiann's house?" Annani asked as they entered the servants' corridor.

"Yes, I did as you asked. I went there last night before going home."

"Did you see Khiann?"

Gulan blushed. "Yes, my lady. But he did not see me. I peeked from the other side of the fence. He was sparring with his squire. Esag."

The way Gulan whispered Esag's name, it was obvious the blush had been all about the squire and not Khiann. Which was a relief. It would have been a shame if poor Gulan fancied the god. Khiann belonged to Annani.

6

ANNANI

"The head cook is nearly blind," Gulan said as she led Annani into Khiann's family's estate kitchen.

"A human. Good, then we do not need to whisper."

"That is why I chose the kitchen as our entry."

The old cook turned to look their way. "How can I help you, young man?"

Gulan blushed profusely. The cook did not see well enough to distinguish her facial features, and given her height he'd assumed she was a male.

"I am Gulan, Lady Annani's maid. My little sister has a school assignment about commerce, and my mistress suggested that I ask Master Khiann's help. She said he is very knowledgeable on the subject. He and my mistress went to school together."

To Gulan's credit, she did not sound timid or hesitant as she usually did. Perhaps it was because the cook was human and therefore not intimidating as far as she was concerned, or because he had made her angry by addressing her as a male.

Hmm, that was an interesting thought. Apparently, angry Gulan was not shy or timid. Perhaps Annani should rile her up on occasion and see if it had the same effect.

The cook waved his big mixing spoon. "The master is out in the yard, training. You can go out and ask him. Your little sister should stay here, out of harm's way. You should be careful too, Gulan. Master Khiann and Master Esag train with sharp weapons."

"I will exercise caution. Thank you for the warning."

He nodded and went back to stirring the stew in his big pot.

Casting Annani one last glance, Gulan sighed before stepping out of the kitchen and leaving her with the cook.

It was difficult for Annani to refrain from talking. Curious by nature, she had a lot of questions she would have loved to ask the old man. Like how he was managing with his poor eyesight. How did he feel about working in Khiann's household? Did Khiann treat him kindly?

The problem was that her voice would have betrayed her as surely as her flaming red hair or her glowing skin. Naturally, she could have thralled the old man to not notice any of it, but a thrall might have been harmful to an aging human brain.

Gods needed to be very careful with their powers, especially when using them on humans. Immortal minds were stronger, and therefore could withstand more, but humans were too fragile for the immense onslaught of godly mental powers when unchecked.

It was all too easy to abuse it, to feel superior to everyone who was not a god and deem them less worthy. But Nai had drilled into Annani's head the importance of treating everyone with care and dignity, even lowly humans. The gods' law protected humans and immortals against being taken advantage of, but that did not mean it was always followed to the letter. Some gods, like Mortdh, believed themselves above the law.

A few minutes later, Khiann rushed into the kitchen with a panic-stricken expression on his face. "What are you doing here?"

Annani pushed to her feet and took his hand. "I need help with a school project, my lord," she whispered to camouflage her voice.

"What?"

Putting a finger to her lips, she tugged on his hand. "Come."

Outside, Gulan was leaning against the kitchen wall and hyperventilating, evidently from the exertion of chasing after Khiann. The girl was a strong runner, but she was no match for a god.

Annani patted her arm. "Everything is fine, Gulan. Go back into the kitchen and rest. Maybe grab something to eat."

"Yes, my lady."

Annani pulled Khiann behind her as she ventured deeper into his estate's gardens.

"Where are you going?"

"Someplace we can talk privately."

"You are out of your mind. What if someone sees us together?"

Annani stopped and turned toward him, craning her neck to look up at his face. He was so tall, one of the tallest men she knew. Funny that a tiny woman like her fancied a big man like him. But maybe that was exactly why she found him so attractive.

Well, not only that. It was just one of many reasons. Khiann was smart and handsome, more so than the other gods despite all of them being perfectly formed. A rotten attitude could mar the most beautiful face, and an inner beauty could make a plain one seem gorgeous.

Not that there was anything plain about Khiann, he was stunning, and yet Annani found his character to be his most attractive feature.

He was not full of himself, he did not think others needed to worship him, and he treated everyone with respect, including humans and immortals.

Annani valued that above all. This god was more worthy than any of the others who deluded themselves into thinking that they were real deities deserving of prayers.

"I do not care if anyone does. It is not against the law for one god to seek the company of another. It is just that as Ahn and Nai's daughter, I am not allowed the same freedoms every other god takes for granted, and therefore I am treated unfairly." She smiled. "You know me, Khiann. Am I the sort of woman who would accept unfair restrictions without a fight?"

He lifted his hand, and for a moment she thought he would caress her cheek, or wrap that big hand of his around the back of her neck to hold her for a kiss, but even though his eyes blazed with the need to touch her, he did none of those things. "You are the future leader of the realm, Annani, you are bound by different rules than the rest of us."

"That might be true, but as a leader, I need to have a mind of my own and effect change when I think change is needed."

Looking despondent, he shook his head. "You are young, and you think with your heart instead of your head. Your intended would not be happy about you arranging clandestine meetings with another male."

Annani looked back at the house. This was not a conversation she wanted anyone to overhear. The cook and Gulan were of no consequence, but an immortal might wander into the kitchen and eavesdrop.

Mortdh had spies everywhere, even she knew it.

It was better he did not learn of her plan until it was too late for him to do anything about it.

"Let us venture deeper into the gardens, Khiann, where we will not be disturbed."

He nodded. "As you wish."

7

GULAN

Gulan leaned her elbows on the kitchen table and propped her heavy head on her hands.

She was going to get whipped even if Annani took the blame. Her only hope was that they would not get caught. If anyone found out that Gulan had helped sneak the princess out of the palace, just the two of them without a guard to escort her, and then let Annani out of her sight while in the company of a young male, she would be shown no mercy.

Not for the first time, Gulan wished she was more assertive and had refused this crazy adventure, the latest one in a long line the princess came up with on a regular basis.

But who was she to say no to Annani when even the royal couple seldom did?

Ever since Gulan became Annani's companion and personal maid, she had watched the princess charm and manipulate to get whatever she wanted. It was impossible to say no to her, not because she was so frightening, but because she was so lovable.

Humans called her the goddess of love, not officially, of course. The title already belonged to a different goddess, whose idea of love was more carnal in nature. Calling Annani by that title would have suggested that she was loose with her favors, which was unbefitting of the future ruler of the realm. Unfortunately, the goddess of wisdom was already taken too, not that it was a good fit for Annani. She was smart but not always wise.

Perhaps the goddess of compassion would have been a good title for her, but as the future ruler she needed something that denoted strength, and compassion was often regarded as weakness.

Oh, well. It was not up to Gulan anyway. She was just a servant.

The cook placed a big bowl of stew in front of her. "If you are sitting in my kitchen, you are eating."

"Thank you, but I have already eaten."

"Nonsense. A big girl like you needs plenty of nourishment. Eat up. And when your little sister comes back, I will give her a bowl of stew as well. I do not want your lady to think we do not know how to welcome guests in this household."

Ugh. She hated when people called her big. As if she needed a reminder. Other immortal girls were blessed with gifts like sharing thoughts without speaking, or the ability to make plants flourish, or even seeing the future on rare occasions, but her gift had to be size and strength.

A wonderful gift for a male, but a curse for a female.

Boys either ignored her or tried to treat her as another boy, until discovering that she did not act boyish at all. Gulan did not like the rough games boys played, and she did not like their crude jokes. She liked pretty dresses and flowers and poetry.

"Hey, Gulan, what are you up to?" Esag startled her.

As soon as she had told Khiann who was waiting for him in the kitchen, he had thralled his squire and sent him away. Esag should not remember her arrival. She could tell him the same story she'd told the cook, but maybe if she acted rude he would leave and she would not have to talk to him at all. That would be best.

"I am eating. What are you doing here?"

He grinned, flashing her a smile that had her heart skip a beat. "This happens to be my home. And this is the kitchen I eat in every day." He sat on a stool next to her. Way too close.

She picked up hers and moved it a little further away.

Esag was still looking at her, waiting for an answer.

With a sigh, she put down her spoon and prepared to lie again. "My little sister has a school project about commerce. My lady suggested that we seek Master Khiann's advice since he is an expert in this field."

Esag eyed her suspiciously. "A school project, eh? What is she supposed to write about?"

Luckily, Annani had been very thorough in taking care of all the little details that had the potential of sabotaging her schemes, including preparing an answer to exactly this question. "She needs to list at least five goods that are brought from the west, and five that are brought from the east, and their mode of transportation. Which goods are ferried by boats using the river routes, and which are brought by caravans over land."

As doubt melted off Esag's face, he shifted on his stool, straightening his back and inflating his chest. "I could have answered those questions for her. There was no need to bother Master Khiann. I know everything he knows. He takes me everywhere he goes."

Was Esag boasting to impress her?

Gulan felt her cheeks warm up.

The cook placed a bowl of stew in front of him, but Esag pushed it aside. "I should relieve Khiann from this task. He has better things to do than helping your little sister with her school project. I should be the one doing that."

Oh, no. He could not go. Annani could shroud herself to look like Tula, but her time with Khiann would be cut short, and she would never forgive Gulan for not stopping the squire.

Reaching for his arm, Gulan swallowed hard as she placed her hand gently on his bicep. "Please stay. I am curious about commerce too. I would love to hear all about it from someone as knowledgeable and well-informed as you."

She had never flirted with a guy before, let alone a handsome one like Esag. It felt incredibly awkward and frightening.

As long as Gulan pretended that she could not care less about men, it did not hurt as much to be ignored. But showing interest, flirting, and then getting brushed off would be painful.

Surprisingly, though, Esag smiled and sat back down. "I guess Khiann can spare a few moments for your sister." He winked. "I would rather spend time with a woman than with a kid."

Oh, dear merciful Fates.

Gulan felt faint.

8

ANNANI

Khiann's family estate garden was almost as big as the one at the palace. Most of it was taken up by vegetables and spices to supply the kitchen, but further away were beds of flowers that had been planted for their beauty, and trees, some of them heavy with fruit and some which had none but were long-limbed and abundant with foliage. Those had been obviously planted for their shade.

Annani found a stone bench under one of those shade-providing beauties and sat down, expecting Khiann to join her, but the stubborn man remained standing.

"I do not bite," she taunted. *Not yet, anyway*. "Would you please sit with me?"

Reluctantly, he did, lowering himself to the furthest spot on the bench, as far away from her as the stretch of stone allowed, which was not far at all. If Tula were there, she could have fit in between them, but Gulan would have been hard pressed to squeeze in.

"You wanted to talk, my lady."

"Annani will do. I am not big on honorifics."

"As you wish."

Now that she had him alone, her bravado faltered. Annani was confident in her beauty, and even though some people found her too impetuous and outspoken, most loved her anyway. But what she wanted from Khiann was a different kind of love, and she could not just order him to feel it.

"I came here to talk to you."

"You already said that."

"I know. But now I am lost for words."

He chuckled. "That is not the Annani I remember from school. You were very vocal."

Aha.

So Khiann had been paying attention while pretending not to.

Just as she had suspected.

With her confidence boosted, Annani regained her footing and decided it was time to tease Khiann and get him to loosen up around her.

She had done the same with her guards, which had provided her with lots of entertainment as well as practice, making her an expert tease. When first assigned to her, the guys had been formal and rigid, kind of like Khiann was now, but she would have none of that. The relentless teasing had worked and they ended up friends and gaming buddies. When no one was looking. Fates forbid her father saw her interact with her guards like that.

Khiann was no different. Too calm and collected for his own good, he needed some rattling. "I see. I know that I am somewhat outspoken. Are you one of those males who like their females demure and subdued?"

His eyes widened. "No. I did not mean it that way. I loved hearing you argue with the teachers. You would get them so angry with your progressive ideas, but they could not order you to be quiet or yell at you or punish you in any way."

She nodded. "I was the voice of rebellion." Not wanting him to think she was argumentative just because she could be, Annani continued. "I find slavery abhorrent. I know our laws protect the rights of slaves, ensuring that they are treated as well as paid servants, but people should not own other people."

Khiann rose to his feet and started pacing in front of the bench.

"What about those who sell themselves into slavery to repay debts or to provide for their impoverished families? And what about the criminals who are sentenced to slavery?"

Ugh, normally she loved debating, but not today. Well, she was going to voice arguments, but not about politics. Well, kind of about politics, since her evil intended was a political choice.

She waved a hand. "I am sure alternative solutions can be found. But I do not wish to discuss social injustice with you. That is not why I came here wearing a disguise and scaring my poor maid who does not approve of my adventurous endeavors."

He stopped and looked down at her.

"Why did you?"

"Because there was no other way for me to talk to you."

"You could have issued a summons."

"Yes, and then Mortdh's spies would have reported it to him right away."

Khiann sighed. "What is it that you want, Annani?"

"You." It was bold, but it was the truth, and she did not have time to play games.

Khiann rubbed his jaw. "As much as I am flattered by the proposal, I have to decline."

Annani's heart sank down to her sandals.

But then he continued, "I do not wish to become the secret lover you keep on the side, and who Mortdh finds a way to dispose of."

Annani was not easily embarrassed. Normally she was the one causing embarrassment, not the other way around, but Khiann's assumption made her cheeks flare with heat.

Not that it was groundless. Gods rarely mated for love, and it was not uncommon for one or both to keep secret lovers that everyone knew about.

However, this was not how Annani saw her future. If she had her way, she would be joined with her true-love mate or not at all.

"Is that what you think I am suggesting?"

He lifted a brow.

"That is not why I am here. I do not seek a lover, one who I would keep while mated to Mortdh."

Khiann shrugged. "It is not that I do not understand. I do. After the mating ceremony, you probably would not even see him until it was time for you to take the throne. You will need a man to warm your bed. But I am not that man. Not because you are undesirable, I do not want you to think that even for a moment, but because…" he hesitated before blurting, "I travel a lot."

Letting his head drop down, he added, "And because I want a mate who would be fully mine. A true-love mate."

Annani stood up and reached for his cheek. At first, he flinched away, but when she kept going, undeterred, he sighed and let her touch him.

"This is what I want too, Khiann. I do not want to mate Mortdh. I would rather mate with a human than that vile god. And I do not have to mate with him. The law states that I can choose my mate, and that my choice supersedes Mortdh's claim. I do not know if you and I are each other's fated, but I know there is a mutual attraction. I would like to give us a chance to find out if there is more."

He closed his eyes and groaned as if she was torturing him.

"I always liked you, Khiann. In school, I could not wait to see you out in the schoolyard, even though you never paid attention to me. I know it does not mean much, but it is a start."

As Khiann opened his eyes, they were blazing with inner light. "It would be the start of a war. Mortdh is powerful and dangerous. The cedar trees trade made him very rich, and up north he has no competition from the other gods. Thanks to him, the local human population thrives, and they worship him and only him. He has thousands of humans and hundreds of immortals who are willing to fight a war at his command."

Did he think she was dumb and had not thought this

all the way through? Sometimes Annani felt like she was the only one who had.

"I know all that. I also know what the future holds if I do nothing. What do you think will happen when my parents step down, and I take the throne together with Mortdh? He is not like the other gods, he is proving it with every step he takes. He does not believe in cooperation or voting. He wants to be the absolute ruler. The first thing he would do is dismiss the large assembly. If I try to stand in his way, he will have me eliminated or imprisoned."

Khiann's fangs elongated, sending shivers down Annani's spine, but she was not sure whether they were caused by anger or desire.

"This is thousands of years in the future," he hissed through his fangs.

"Perhaps. But in the meantime, Mortdh keeps growing stronger, not weaker. He will become invincible."

Annani took Khiann's hand, clasping it in both of hers. "We got carried away. I am here not because of politics, but because my heart tells me to take a chance on love. That being said, I am not as selfish and irresponsible as you might think. In my opinion, it is better to start a war now, when we can still win it, than wait until it is too late."

9

KHIANN

As Annani's eyes beseeched him to take a monumental chance on her, Khiann wondered whether the driving force behind her bold move was desperation or yearning for love.

Perhaps it was both.

He could not fault Annani for seeking a way to avoid mating with Mortdh. But he could not help questioning her motives. Had she turned to him because she had true feelings for him, or because he had happened to be in the right place at the right time?

If not for his audience with Ahn, would Annani have remembered him at all? Would she have gone after any unmated god?

How could he determine the truth?

And even if Annani was truly motivated by love, or rather by the hope of finding it with him, was he willing to start a war over her, and could love mitigate his culpability?

If Annani was the one, he could live with the guilt for a true-love mate.

He had yearned for her for years, lusted after her, but a true-love mating was about more than lust.

What if they were both just infatuated with each other?

What if they started a war for nothing?

But then Annani had been right in her assessment of Mortdh, his future plans, and his current chances, or lack thereof, of winning a war.

Khiann had often voiced similar opinions when talking with his father.

But for some reason, the older generation of gods was not as concerned with Mortdh amassing power in the north. After thousands of years of peaceful coexistence, no one considered war a possibility.

Maybe they were right. Maybe Mortdh would not start a war over Annani.

Or perhaps he would.

Fates help me.

"Khiann." Annani tugged on his hand.

"Yes?"

"Well?"

He smoothed his palm over his hair. "Tell me what you want me to do, Annani."

She blushed. "I want you to kiss me."

"What?" He almost choked on his own saliva.

Annani glanced at him from under lowered lashes. "I have never been kissed."

His eyes went straight to her mouth. Fates, those lips were made for kissing, and it was a crime that they had never been. By him.

"I cannot."

Her blush deepened, and she lowered her head.

He hooked a finger under her chin, lifting her head back up. "But you can. I cannot refuse the princess." Technically, he had to obey her commands. He would not be breaking any laws, written or implied, if he let her kiss him.

Annani smiled, her tiny fangs gleaming white.

Fates, how he wished to feel her bite on his skin. Would she be as wild and as ferocious as he imagined?

"You are too tall for me to reach. If I am to kiss you, you need to sit down."

His butt dropped on the bench before she finished her sentence.

Annani approached him with the sinuous fluidity of a seductress, not an innocent girl of seventeen summers who had never been kissed. She sat on his lap and wrapped her arms around his neck, her eyes hooded with desire and blazing blue-green light. "I think this will work."

Pulling on his neck, she brought his head down.

The moment she touched her sweet lips to his, in a kiss that was almost chaste, he became lightheaded, probably because all the blood in his body rushed down into his manhood.

Even as inexperienced as she was, Annani obviously knew what the hardness she was feeling through her thin tunic meant because she wiggled in his lap, making matters even worse.

She lifted her lips and smiled. "I do not know what I am doing, but apparently it is working."

The girl needed him to show her how it was done. "Command me to kiss you."

Her eyes widening, it took her a moment before understanding dawned. "Khiann son of Navohn, I command you to kiss me."

Lifting his hand to her nape, he intended only to hold her for his kiss, but she was so small and slender that his fingers almost completely encircled her throat. He moved his hand up, gently cradling the entire back of her head, then stroked her mouth with his, getting her accustomed to his touch before licking at the seam of her lips.

On a moan, Annani opened her mouth.

As Khiann eased his tongue into her sweetness, he was not prepared for the onslaught of sensations. He was drowning in them, dizzy with pleasure and need, losing his mind in the fire Annani was igniting in his loins.

Had anything ever felt like that?

Boneless in his arms, her small body melting into his chest, Annani seemed just as lost as he was.

With the scent of her desire bombarding his senses, the last of his control was wrestled away from his grasp, and he smashed his mouth over hers, his tongue spearing into her the way he would one day make love to her, claiming her.

Annani belonged to him. They belonged together. If he had doubts before, they were now gone because this kiss was unlike any Khiann had had before.

He must have nicked her with his fangs, and when the taste of her blood exploded in his mouth, he was ready to go to war for her. No matter what he had to do, he was never letting go. If need be, he would exchange his merchant's ledger for a shield and his stylus for a spear and become a warrior.

Licking her lips, he healed the small hurt he had caused.

"You are mine," he hissed.

Her eyes hooded with desire, unfocused, her lips parted, soft and puffy from his kiss, she touched a finger to where his mouth had been a moment ago.

Without thinking, he closed his palm over her nape, and applied a little pressure. "Say it." Khiann didn't know what possessed him to act that way. And with none other than the princess of the realm. The rational, cautious, and courteous man was gone, overtaken by a mindless beast.

"I am yours," Annani mumbled, then a big grin split her face. "And you are mine, Khiann son of Navohn. Our pact is sealed by the power of the greatest kiss that ever was and ever will be. Except, of course, for our second one, and the third, and the fourth..."

10

ANNANI

With trembling hands, Khiann lifted Annani off his lap and set her down next to him. A shame, since she was not done kissing him. She wanted a lifetime of kisses like that.

"Why did you stop?" she asked.

It took him a moment to stabilize his ragged breathing. "Because if I continued, I would not have stopped at kissing." He leaned his elbows on his knees and let his head hang down from his shoulders.

Why did he appear so defeated?

Annani had a pretty good idea what he had meant, and the images appearing in her head made her regret the loss of his touch even more. She was a woman with a woman's needs, and Khiann was who she wanted to satisfy them. No one else.

"I would not have minded that at all."

Khiann turned his head and looked up at her, his eyes so full of longing that her breath caught in her throat. Being wanted like that brought about an unexpected rush. She was powerful, and not only because she was the princess, but because her power came from her femininity and the desire it evoked.

Her mother had failed to tell her that. It was a shame Nai was such a serious woman. If she had one-tenth of Annani's humor, they could have enjoyed each other's company so much more. As it was, Nai was more concerned with teaching her daughter all about ruling than even a little bit about what it meant to be a woman.

Khiann reached for her hand and clasped it in his big one. "I want you so much that it hurts, but I cannot have you. I would be putting my entire family in jeopardy. Mortdh is not the only one who would want my head, your father would too, and he would not stop with mine only. He would consider the seduction of his only daughter an act of treason."

Annani had no idea what Khiann was talking about, and why he was so afraid. No one would take the head of a god. It was not allowed. The worst punishment possible for a god was entombment, and it had not been done even once in their history.

"You are making a storm out of a gentle breeze. First of all, I am seducing you, and not the other way around."

Khiann chuckled as if she had told a joke. "Right."

Annani got to her feet, put her hands on her hips, and glared at the man. "Are we sitting in the palace's garden, after you snuck in to see me, or are we sitting in your parents' estate gardens after I went to considerable trouble to come and see you? I am the one doing the seducing here."

Khiann lifted his hands in surrender. "Peace, little tigress. I am not belittling the courage it took for you to come to me. I am quite impressed. But if I let it go any further than one kiss, the blame would be mine. I cannot claim I was a helpless victim in this, now can I?"

The truth was on his side, and so was the law.

When Annani's father had taken her mother, who was not of age at the time, it had not mattered that Nai had seduced him quite deliberately.

Ahn had wiggled out of severe punishment by mating Nai and vowing to remain faithful to her. A big concession coming from a ruler who typically entertained a horde of concubines and mistresses.

It turned out they were each other's fated mates, so the vow had not been necessary, but neither of them had known that when Nai had done the seducing and Ahn had done the succumbing. Nai wanted to mate with the most powerful god, and Ahn wanted to bed a beautiful girl. The rest was history.

Still, Ahn had never attempted to claim innocence. He'd acknowledged his crime, publicly, and had been willing to pay the price.

Letting out a puff of air, Annani sat back down. "I am not interested in a clandestine affair behind my father's back. I want everything to be out in the open. I am still unmated, and therefore free to choose my suitor."

His eyes widened. "You want me to come to the palace and ask your father's permission to court you?"

"Of course. What else did you think I wanted?"

Khiann rubbed his jaw. "I thought you wanted to find out if we are fated mates first."

Annani sighed. "I wish I had the luxury to take my time and make certain we are true-love mates before committing to this course of action, but my situation does not allow for it. Still, I strongly believe that we are." She looked at him from under her lashes. "I might be inexperienced, but I think our kiss was not like other kisses. It was a life-altering experience. Do you agree?"

His eyes smoldering with desire, he reached for her, pulling her into his lap again. "It should be recorded in the annals of history as the one to outdo them all."

Annani cast Khiann a seductive look, hoping she was doing it right and not making a fool of herself. "Perhaps we should try another kiss? Just to make sure that we did not imagine it to be more than it was?"

Hesitating only for a moment, Khiann cupped the back of her head and slowly leaned forward.

Annani's heart started pounding against her rib cage as if it wanted to break free from the confinement of her chest and jump into Khiann's.

But as his lips touched hers softly, her heart slowed down and she closed her eyes. His scent enveloped her like a cocoon, manly, seductive, addictive. She breathed him in, pressing her body against his powerful chest, her pebbled nipples seeking contact, aching for friction.

Khiann's control was admirable.

Instead of devouring her with the hunger she could feel in his coiled muscles, his mouth moved slowly over hers, his tongue flicking gently along the seam of her lips but not seeking entry.

Not yet.

Was he afraid of nicking her with his fangs again?

She didn't mind. There was something deeply erotic about her blood coating his tongue with her essence, and about the small hurt and the tender way he licked it away.

Parting her lips, she leaned into him, and let herself get lost in the sensations. As he accepted her invitation and slid his tongue between her parted lips, she rewarded him with a moan that started deep in her throat and ended up in his mouth.

Desperate for more, hungry for his touch, she undulated her hips, rubbing her core against his hardness in a futile attempt to seek relief.

With a groan, Khiann wrapped his arm around her waist, halting her gyrations.

When she mewled in protest, he gentled her, rubbing small circles on her back, kissing her forehead, her eyelids, the bridge of her nose.

Annani sighed and put her cheek on his chest, listening to the rapid beat of his heart. "Are you convinced now?"

He kept rubbing. "I did not need convincing. I know you are the one for me."

If he knew, why had he been fighting her so hard? Was it fear of Mortdh? Or fear of Ahn?

"Will you come to talk with my father?"

"I have to consult with mine first. My actions will have an impact on my entire family."

Annani lifted her head and looked into Khiann's eyes. "You are not alone in this. I will work on my father from the other end. Between the two of us, we can convince him that letting you court me is a brilliant idea."

Khiann snorted. "Please, enlighten me. Because all I can see is how this will end up in a war."

"I will consult with my uncle Ekin. He is the smartest god I know."

Khiann was taken aback, his eyes narrowing and his brows dipping low. "Ekin? Mortdh's father?"

"Do not worry. He is not going to tell Mortdh."

"Why would he help you against his son?"

"Ekin is not happy about Mortdh's ambitions, and he is not happy about my father promising me to his son. He knows Mortdh is not right in the head. Not as in stupid, unfortunately, he has inherited his father's smarts, but in other ways. He is insane."

Khiann looked uncomfortable for a moment. "I do not know how to tell you this, but Ekin was probably disappointed your father did not promise you to him. After all, Ekin is the older brother, and if he were not the son of a concubine instead of the official mate, he would have been the ruler."

Annani grimaced and waved a hand. "Do not say things like that. Ekin held me when I was a baby, he played with me when I was a toddler, and he told me stories when I was a little kid. He sees me as a daughter, not as a possible mate."

"That might be true, but you know political considerations have nothing to do with matters of the heart."

"Ekin is not power hungry, and he is not interested in politics. He loves being a scientist and an inventor. He would refuse leadership even if it were handed to him on a golden platter."

11

GULAN

"What I love most about being Khiann's squire is the travel. I get to see the world." Esag lifted a pitcher of beer to those fleshy lips of his and took a large gulp.

Gulan had been trying her best to pay attention to his stories instead of staring at his mouth and imagining how it would feel to be kissed by him, but it was no use. Esag had the most beautiful lips she had ever seen on a male.

Lucky for her, he was probably thinking that she was staring at his mouth because she found him so fascinating. And maybe he was. She would have known if she had heard more than one or two words of every other sentence.

"Do not get me wrong, Khiann is a great guy, and we have been friends since the first day I started working for him, so it is not all about the travel. I would have loved being his squire even if he were one of those gods who just wants to be worshiped and pampered, but traveling with him is a big bonus. I especially love sailing the rivers, but the caravans are fun too."

"Esag!" Khiann called from the doorway. "I need to show you something."

"Yes, my lord." Esag pushed to his feet. "It was nice talking to you, Gulan. I hope you and your sister come visit again." He leaned closer, his proximity and his scent making her feel faint. "You can also come without your sister." He winked.

"Esag! I am waiting!" Khiann called again.

Esag straightened to his full height, which was quite impressive. He was one of the few men who were taller than her. "I have to go. See you around, Gulan."

Feeling like an idiot, she nodded. During the entire time they had spent together, she had not said more than a handful of sentences, while Esag had done all the talking. She was not great with words to begin with, but he had made her completely tongue-tied.

As soon as Esag left with Khiann, Annani slunk into the kitchen.

"I am ready to go, Gulan," she whispered loudly, masking her voice. "I have all I need for my school report."

The cook turned to her. "Would you like a bowl of stew before you depart, young lady?"

Gulan stood up and took Annani's hand as if she really was Tula. "Thank you for your kind offer, but our mother awaits our return. We have tarried long enough as it is."

"Next time, then."

"I thank you kindly."

Still holding on to Annani's hand, Gulan walked

over to the cook and inclined her head. "Thank you for the stew. It was lovely."

"I am glad." He patted her arm. "But I am sure it was not half as lovely as Master Esag's company."

Gulan felt her cheeks get even hotter than they had been for the past hour, which meant they were about to catch fire. "Thank you again for the meal."

Tugging her shawl lower to cover more of her face, Annani giggled and whispered quietly, "I see both of us had fun." She wrapped her arm around Gulan's waist and headed out.

As soon as they were out on the street, the goddess sighed dramatically. "I always wondered about my first kiss. Who would I do it with? How would it feel? Would I like it? Would I want more? But I never imagined it would shake the earth under my sandals and spin my head."

Gulan grimaced. "It sounds a lot like being drunk, and this is not what I would call fun." Her words had sounded bitter even to her own ears, but for once she could not hold it in and pretend she was not envious.

Annani, who was a year younger than her, had already gotten her first kiss even though she was the princess, guarded and sequestered like no other girl, goddess, immortal, or human.

Most second- and third-generation immortal girls got their first kiss during the transition ceremony. Born mortal, they had to be bitten by an immortal male and injected with his venom in order to transition into immortality. The act was sexual in nature, enjoyed between immortal couples, but because it had to be done at the onset of puberty, it was usually accompanied by nothing more than a kiss. Or in Gulan's case, nothing at all.

The boy her family had secured for the ceremony had only bitten her, he had not kissed her, which had been a major blow to Gulan's self-confidence. A kiss was not required, but it was kind of expected. Unless the girl was taller than most grown men and lacked feminine grace.

Gulan's growth had been so rapid, that she had constantly been trying to catch up and get used to her new size. Thank the merciful Fates she'd stopped growing at fifteen and was no longer as ungainly as she used to be.

She should not complain, though.

The Fates who had gifted her with that particular set of attributes had not been cruel. Gulan's size combined with her gentle nature had gotten her the coveted position as the princess's personal maid and companion. Her family was certainly grateful for the generous wages she had been bringing home since she was twelve.

Annani sighed. "Oh, Gulan, if that is how being drunk feels it is no wonder beer is so popular. That kiss was magical."

With Annani shrouding herself in Tula's image, they got back into the palace undetected, sneaking through the servants' entrance. To know it was the goddess wearing her sister's image like a costume was unnerving to say the least.

Annani kept the shroud until they were safely inside her room.

Tula sat up. "How did it go?"

The princess cast the shawl aside and twirled. "Amazing. I got my first kiss."

"Wow." Clutching the blanket to her chest, Tula was wide-eyed. "Did you like it?"

"I loved it. The best thing that ever happened to me, and hopefully there will be many more kisses." She winked at Gulan before sauntering behind the partition.

"Did anyone come in?" Annani asked as she threw Tula's tunic over the top of it.

"No. I actually fell asleep. Your bed is heavenly, my lady."

Gulan handed Annani a new dress. "What is next? Are we going to sneak out like that every day?"

"There is no further need for that. I convinced Khiann to ask my father's permission to court me. If we sneak around, it will be probably in the palace's gardens to steal kisses."

"Good. Today was nerve-wracking." Gulan tossed Tula's tunic on the bed. "Get dressed. We need to get you home."

She was going to pray to the Fates for Ahn to approve Khiann's courtship. The odds were against that ever coming to pass, but to keep her sanity, Gulan would beseech the Fates on Annani's behalf.

Maybe with the young goddess busy kissing her chosen one in the palace's gardens, she would not have time to come up with any new schemes.

Annani emerged from behind the screen, looking regal again. "I want to thank you both for your help." She walked over to her jewelry chest.

"This is for you, Gulan." She handed her a necklace made of gold and precious stones. "And this is for you."

She handed Tula a bracelet made from the same materials.

Each of the items could feed a large human family for a year.

"It is too much, my lady. We cannot accept such great gifts." Gulan tried to return the necklace.

Casting her an evil glare, Tula cradled the bracelet in her hands.

Annani arched one perfectly shaped red brow and pushed Gulan's hand away. "You would offend me by refusing my gifts?"

Ugh, the goddess was impossible, always twisting things around to get her way. "Of course not, my lady."

Annani grinned. "Very well. I will see you bright and early tomorrow morning, Gulan. Tonight, I am going to dream of passionate kisses, and tomorrow I am going to come up with a plan to convince my father that Khiann is not only the best choice for me, but also for the future of the realm."

PART 2

SECRET ACCORD

1

KHIANN

Thoughts of Annani had kept Khiann awake most of the night—elation warring with anxiety, hope dueling with despair. When temptation finally did away with caution, the moon was still high in the sky.

Giving up on getting any sleep, Khiann got up and walked over to the stone basin. Perhaps a splash of cold water on his face would help clear his mind.

He needed advice, and he needed help.

A young god just starting out in the world had no access to the ruler or even his assistants, but his father was one of the ancients, and as such in a position to gain Ahn's ear.

Navohn was one of a handful of gods who could claim that privilege.

The question was whether his father would agree to help. Probably not. Annani's proposal was the best and the worst thing to ever happen to Khiann. On the one hand was the possibility of endless bliss with his truelove mate. On the other hand was war and possible retaliation against his family. If he were in his father's sandals, he would refuse without giving it a second thought.

But who knew? Navohn was a good-natured god and the best possible father. His love for Khiann might influence his decision. Or perhaps his deep dislike for Mortdh would be the deciding factor.

In either case, there was hope.

It would be some time before Navohn awakened and started his workday. In the meantime, Khiann needed to come up with the best way of presenting Annani's proposal and its ramifications.

She was so courageous for taking the initiative and coming to him with her bold offer. Khiann felt humbled and disappointed in himself for not being the one to go to her first. After all, he had desired Annani for years. What a shame that he had convinced himself there was no chance of him ever winning her hand.

From now on, though, he would fight for her.

For them.

Navohn was leaving on a trade expedition in nine days and was in the midst of intense preparations, which meant that time was of the essence. Preparing a caravan for the road was a more complicated task than people thought, and on top of that, his father was trying to cram all of his knowledge into Khiann's head before leaving.

It was not a good time for such an important talk, but it would be weeks before his father returned and Annani was not a patient goddess. She might do something foolish if Khiann didn't act fast enough.

When dawn finally arrived, he strode into Navohn's office, which he now shared. "I need to discuss an important matter with you, Father."

"Of course. What is it about? Are you worried about being left in charge for the first time?"

Up until now, his father had taken Khiann along on his travels, leaving behind a trusted assistant to look after their business affairs. This time, however, the assistant was going with Navohn, and Khiann was staying behind to manage the office. A big responsibility, but he was ready.

Mostly.

"It is not that. Although, yes, I am somewhat apprehensive. But trade is not what I wanted to talk to you about. It is something bigger than that."

Navohn's expression turned from curious to worried, and a deep furrow appeared between his brows. "Do not tell me that you are considering Ahn's suggestion to apply for the leadership of a city-state?"

"No, I am not interested in that way of life. Although I might have to reconsider."

His father's eyes narrowed in a rare display of agitation. "I do not understand. You are contradicting yourself, son."

Khiann wished there was some elegant way to lead up to what he needed to ask, but the many hours he had spent debating with himself had produced nothing. He was not as sophisticated or as experienced in negotiations as his father, who was a master at painting pictures and feelings with his words and his subtle gestures. It would be many years before Khiann became as eloquent.

But then he was not dealing with a client. His father loved him and would forgive a blunt delivery. To save time, it would be best to just come out with it.

"Before I continue, I need to ensure that our conversation is private. With your permission, I will take care of this."

His father nodded. "Now you really have me worried," he said as Khiann cast a soundproofing shroud around the office.

"Annani came to see me yesterday."

"Annani? As in Princess Annani?"

"There is only one. Yes, Ahn's daughter garbed herself in a commoner's attire and sneaked out of the palace to see me. She wants me to ask her father's permission to court her."

Navohn could not have been more shocked if he had told him that the boat of a million years had come back to take the gods home.

"The princess is promised to Mortdh."

Khiann rubbed his brows between two fingers. "Tell me something I do not know. This is the reason she came to me wearing a disguise. Mortdh's spies are everywhere, and the princess is desperate to escape the fate of one day being forced to join him."

With a sigh, Navohn didn't so much lean back as slump in his chair. "I do not blame her. Her father made a grave mistake by promising her to Mortdh. But in Ahn's defense, seventeen years ago, when Annani was born, Mortdh's ambitions seemed more reasonable and his madness not as apparent."

"Do you think Ahn knows he made a mistake?"

"I am not sure. As long as there is peace, Ahn probably believes it was the right move, even if it means Annani's misery. He is a ruler first and a father second."

"The peace is not going to last long. As soon as Mortdh amasses enough power he is going to attack."

Navohn sighed. "But he is not attacking right now. Even gods and immortals with their long lives and the perspective of history are sometimes blindsided by wishful thinking. Besides, it is not guaranteed that he will indeed attack. Perhaps he will wait patiently for Ahn to step down, mate with Annani, and take the throne peacefully. This is always a possibility."

"Then why is he building an army?"

"Ah, good question. If you believe Mortdh, he needs the army to protect his people against bandit tribes and to secure his cedar trees trade."

"But you do not believe him."

Navohn shook his head. "There are rumors that he is building a huge new temple for himself. Bigger than Ahn's palace."

Khiann scratched his head. "And that means exactly what? Gods love their temples, and the bigger, the better. I do not see the significance of Mortdh building one for himself."

A small smile lifted Navohn's lips. "His big new temple sits on top of a much larger platform which is built from enormous stones. A platform like this is not needed as a foundation for a building, not even one of gigantic proportion. There is only one reason to invest so much effort and resources into building it, and it is not to have chariot races on the temple grounds."

"Do you think he is building a launch pad?"

"What else?" Navohn lifted the pitcher, poured water into two cups, and handed one to Khiann.

"Thank you."

That was troubling news.

As one of the older gods, his father possessed knowledge most of the younger gods did not, and he had passed some of it to Khiann, swearing him to secrecy.

The original gods who had made this place their home had not originated from earth. The space boat that they had arrived in had been orbiting earth for thousands of years, and rockets had been used to transport supplies and ores up to it. That vessel had long departed, and it was probably never coming back. There was no reason for the few small airboats that had remained in the gods' possession and were still functional to clear the atmosphere, and therefore there was no more use for rockets to propel them.

"What does he need a launch pad for?"

"He either wants to venture out into space and explore, or he is planning an annihilation. Rockets can be used for more than launching boats into the outer atmosphere. They can also carry weapons of mass destruction."

A chill ran down Khiann's spine. He had not known that. "Do you know if he has any functioning rockets?"

Navohn spread his arms. "No one knows. But it is not unreasonable to assume that parts can be collected from several broken rockets to construct a new one. My only hope is that nobody in Mortdh's stronghold knows how to do it."

"His father does."

"Ekin is not going to aid Mortdh."

"What makes you say that?"

Navohn took a few long sips of water before putting his cup down on the low table between them. "For all his many faults, Ekin loves humanity and would never do anything to endanger it. He and Mortdh are not even on speaking terms. Ever since Ekin chose Toven as his heir and successor, Mortdh severed all ties to his father."

Toven was the younger brother, and by law second in line after Mortdh, but he had always been Ekin's favorite. Toven was a brilliant scientist and thinker like his father, and just like Ekin, he was uninterested in politics. He was well-liked and respected, unlike Mortdh who was despised and feared.

"That is certainly a relief." Mortdh's ambition combined with his father's brilliance and knowledge would have created a foe too powerful to imagine.

"Indeed. We are very lucky that Ekin has no political aspirations and is concerned only with creation as opposed to destruction."

Khiann chuckled. "From what I hear, his main endeavor is creating more children." If the rumors were true, the god had bedded every available immortal female he could seduce and was warming the beds of several mated goddesses.

Navohn nodded. "As I said before, Ekin has many faults, philandering being just one of them, and yet we are all better off for having him on our side. Imagine what our world would have been like without his many inventions."

"Barely inhabitable. Ekin possesses an incredible mind."

But Ekin and his inventions was not what Khiann wanted to talk about. "What about the princess? Do I have your permission to approach Ahn about her?"

Navohn rubbed his chin between his thumb and forefinger. "Not without me and your mother. You will have to wait for my return."

"The princess is not a patient woman."

His father smiled. "She has quite a reputation. No wonder you are so taken with her. But you will have to explain to the young lady that good things are worth waiting for. During my travels, I will think of the best way to approach Ahn. I have known our ruler for a very long time, and I know the way his mind works."

Annani would not wait patiently for Navohn to return from his trip.

"Is it possible for you to approach Ahn before your departure? I am afraid of what the princess will do if forced to wait."

His father smiled and leaned forward to pat Khiann's shoulder. "I understand. The young have no patience. And you are right. The princess is impetuous and might do something foolish. I will ponder the problem for a day or two and let you know."

Khiann bowed his head. "I am most grateful, Father."

2

ANNANI

"How do I look?" Annani asked Gulan.

"You are as beautiful and as regal as always, my lady."

Did her maid just roll her eyes at Annani's reflection in the mirror?

"What is troubling you? Am I asking this question too often?"

A look of fear skittered across Gulan's face. "No, of course not, my lady. It is just that there is no point to your inquiry. You are always going to get the same answer from me and anyone else you ask."

That was true. But was it because they would not dare give her another answer, or because it was really what they thought?

Annani did not lack confidence, but she knew she was not perfect. For one, she was ridiculously short, which made her look much younger than her seventeen summers, which in turn meant that she was not always taken seriously. But then, it might have more to do with her mischievous behavior than with her looks. Secondly, she was not as well-endowed as Gulan in the breast department. Hers were perky but not voluptuous. Also, her legs were too skinny, and she lacked feminine hips, and her fingers were too short. Her hands looked like they belonged to a twelve-year-old.

So yes, her face was beautiful, and her red hair was magnificent, but there were certain things she would have liked to change about her appearance. Mainly her height. Her other shortcomings were not as troublesome as her diminutive stature. Especially since Khiann was so tall. The top of her head barely reached his collarbone.

Except, unless she had misread his reactions, he found her desirable, and that was the only thing that mattered. If her lack of height did not bother him, why should it bother her?

Annani shrugged at her reflection. "I want to look nice when I go to see Ekin. I need his advice."

"Are you going to return his tablet?" Gulan finished pinning parts of Annani's hair on top of her head, creating an elaborate partial up-do that left most of the tresses loose and hanging down Annani's back.

"This is the pretext I am using."

Gulan went down to her knees to tie the straps of Annani's sandals around her ankles. "You are ready, my lady."

"Thank you. Shall we go?"

With quick hands, the girl twisted her own dark hair into a braid of sorts and pinned it to one side. "I am, my lady."

As always, Annani found Ekin at his study, poring

over the large tablet he used for making schematic drawings.

"What are you working on, Uncle?"

Ekin straightened his back and smiled at her. "These are modifications to the irrigation system. I had a dream last night that gave me an idea how to improve it. You see…" He launched into a long explanation, pointing at this and that on his tablet.

Annani smiled and nodded as if she understood what he was talking about, but the truth was that he had lost her after the second sentence. Ekin used too many technical terms that she was not familiar with, and he was talking too fast. The god was so smart, and his brain worked so fast, that people could not follow his explanations. Most of the time he did not bother, but for some reason, he always tried to explain the most difficult things to her.

Perhaps he believed her to be smarter than she actually was.

It was flattering, and Annani did not wish to change his good opinion of her, so most of the time she did her best to listen. Not today, though, she was too preoccupied and perturbed to pay attention.

Nevertheless, Annani continued to nod and smile. Other than her and his son Toven, who was gone on one of his exploration expeditions, Ekin had no one else to share his exciting news with.

No wonder her uncle's social interactions were limited to bedding as many females as possible. That was the only way he could communicate with those not as smart as he.

Naturally, Ekin had a different explanation for his

philandering. He claimed that he was not mated because he had too much love in him to limit himself to one woman. He needed to spread it around and bring happiness to many.

It sounded silly, but maybe there was some truth to it.

After all, her father, who was utterly loyal and devoted to her mother, did not have as much love in him as his half-brother. Ahn lacked Ekin's joy and charming personality. Perhaps he had just enough love in him to make one woman happy.

She wondered which type her Khiann resembled more.

Hopefully neither. Ahn was too serious and controlling, and Ekin could never be satisfied with only one woman. The god was mated to his science and in love with his inventions.

But Ekin and Ahn were such polar opposites that perhaps Khiann could be a happy medium. Loyal, but not a stickler for the rules, devoted, but not staid, dedicated but still charming…

"Annani!" Ekin snapped his fingers in front of her face. "Are you even paying attention?"

"I am sorry, Uncle. But you lost me. This is too complicated for me."

Ekin shook his head. "You are a very smart young goddess, and if you put your mind to it, you could have understood everything I was explaining. But your head was somewhere else, was it not?"

She lowered her head respectfully. "My apologies, Uncle. You are right. I was thinking of something else."

He lifted a brow and smiled. "Something or

someone?"

Annani felt herself blush. Even though Ekin was not on good terms with his son Mortdh, it was still hard for her to admit that she desired someone else. Except, that was the reason she was here, to ask the smartest god she knew for advice.

"You guessed right, Uncle. There is a young god I fancy." She looked down at her sandals, pretending to admire the intricate knots Gulan had made. "And he is not my intended."

Ekin patted her shoulder. "Come sit with me, child, and tell me what troubles you."

"Thank you." She followed him to the comfortable divan he kept in his study and often took naps on.

According to Ekin, some of his best ideas had come to him while sleeping on it.

"Who is this lucky young god you like?"

As Annani hesitated for a moment, Ekin's wise eyes narrowed at her. "Do not be afraid to confide in me. If I had any say in it, Mortdh would never be allowed anywhere near you. You are pure sunshine and love, while he is consumed by darkness. I will do all I can to aid you."

Annani felt her shoulders sag in relief. "Thank you. I do need all the help I can get." She took a deep breath. "His name is Khiann, son of Navohn."

"Ah, the merchant's son. Good choice."

"You really think so? You do not mind that he has chosen a different path than the one expected of gods?"

Ekin laughed. "You forget who you are talking to, child. Am I sitting in a temple, while my devoted worshipers take care of all my needs?"

"You have a point there. I never stopped to think that what you do is unusual too. But you are a creator, an inventor, and you make everyone's life better. Humans, immortals, and gods are all grateful to you."

"That is true. But to some extent Navohn does it too. He brings goods from faraway lands, and that is making everyone's lives better as well. I have known him for many years, and I have a lot of respect for him. It takes courage to choose a different path. If his son is anything like the father, then you have my blessing."

Having Ekin's blessing was wonderful, but she needed more than that. "Do you think my father will give his blessing too?"

The smile melted off Ekin's face. "My brother is a stubborn god and set in his ways. Once he makes a decision, it is impossible to change his mind. Fates know I tried and failed numerous times."

That was extremely discouraging. If Ekin had been unsuccessful in swaying Ahn's opinion or influencing his decisions, no one else could.

"You are the smartest god I know. If you cannot help me, I do not know who can."

Ekin shook his head. "You have a much better chance than I do. After all, you are his daughter, and he loves you. Ahn has no love for me. But you will need to be very clever about it."

"Would you help me?"

"Of course I will." He squared his shoulders. "I am the champion of love."

Annani felt her heart grow lighter. "What should I do?"

3

KHIANN

"It is no use." Khiann threw his sword on the floor and put his hands on his hips.

To his great shame, Esag had bested him time and again, not because his squire had suddenly become a master swordsman, but because Khiann's head was not in the practice session. It was somewhere up in the clouds.

Annani's kiss had destroyed him, it had changed him.

It was unheard of for a god to lose to an immortal. Unless said god could think of nothing else but tasting a goddess's sweet lips again.

Every time Khiann thought about Annani sitting in his lap, her small body plastered against his, her soft hands roaming his back, he got uncomfortably hard—which apparently was not conducive to winning against a trained immortal opponent.

Fates, he needed to see her again.

Waiting for his father to come up with a plan was

challenging, especially since he was consumed with worry.

What if she was just as impatient as he?

Annani did not possess his restraint. She would once again sneak out of the palace with only Gulan as her bodyguard and put herself and her maid in danger.

She was such a tiny thing. What if she was attacked by bandits?

They could put a knife to her throat and do despicable things to her. Even though Annani was a powerful goddess, she was also young and inexperienced. She would panic. A goddess's only real defense was her ability to thrall her attackers, but thralling required concentration which would be impossible for her under duress.

Gods trained for years to keep a cool head in dangerous situations. Their greater physical strength was good against two or three assailants, but thwarting an attack by more than that required massive mind manipulation. It was their best weapon.

"Khiann, what is going on in your head? Esag took a step back, collecting the practice sword while retreating. "You look like you are ready to tear somebody's throat out."

Camel droppings. Khiann could feel his fangs scraping against his lower lip and venom dripping down his chin.

"I have to see her." He wiped his mouth with the back of his hand. "If I do not, she might come here again, and Fates only know what could happen to her on the way."

Esag frowned. "Who are you talking about?"

Donkey dung. He had forgotten that Esag had not encountered Annani. His squire had seen Gulan and Tula, her little sister, whose visage Annani had shrouded herself in.

"Tula. She might need more help with her school project."

Esag lifted a brow. "Worry for Tula got you so upset?"

"I was thinking of how dangerous it can be for a little girl on the streets. She could get attacked by bandits, or taunted by older boys. It is not safe for her to travel across the city to see me."

"She will not come alone. Gulan will keep her safe."

Khiann waved a hand. "Gulan is not a warrior. She might be strong, but she has no fighting skills. If attacked by humans, she will panic and will not be able to thrall them. Other immortals would probably not threaten her physically, but they might intimidate her and her little sister."

"If you so wish, I can go get Tula and bring her over here. She will be safe with me." Esag sounded eager to go.

Khiann considered his options.

Obviously, Esag's enthusiasm had nothing to do with Tula and everything to do with Gulan. For some reason, the squire fancied Annani's maid. Perhaps Khiann could use this to his advantage.

On the other hand, he should not encourage Esag's behavior. The squire was promised to another, and it was not fair for him to lead Gulan on.

Nothing good would come of it.

But then he was not sending him to flirt with the girl. He could even warn him not to do it.

If Khiann played it right, he could use Tula to see Annani. "Gulan would not want Tula to go alone with you. She would want to accompany her little sister, but she is at the palace serving Annani. What you can do is go there and tell Gulan that I am willing to come to the palace and answer Tula's questions. She can have someone bring her little sister. I am sure her lady would not mind if we use the gardens for our lessons."

Esag regarded him with narrowed eyes. "I find it odd that you care so much about Tula's school project."

The lie came easily. "It is a matter of pride. The girl is going to tell her teacher that I am her source of information. Imagine how bad it will look for me if she does poorly on her assignment."

The story seemed to satisfy Esag. "I understand. Do you want me to go right now and tell Gulan that you want to see Tula today? Or would you prefer to arrange a meeting for tomorrow?"

"You know me. I prefer to take care of things sooner than later. But it is up to her lady. I hope she allows it. I have to abide by her wishes."

His squire dipped his head in a perfunctory bow. "I shall be on my way."

"Thank you."

After Esag had left, Khiann washed up, put a fresh tunic on, and headed for his father's office.

"May I have a word with you?"

"Certainly, come in." Navohn beckoned him to enter.

Khiann glanced at his father's assistant. What he

wanted to talk about was not for the immortal's ears. "Perhaps I should come later."

Navohn waved a hand. "Azar and I are done for now. Come in and take a seat. There are several things I need to discuss with you."

The assistant got to his feet and bowed. "I shall count the barrels as you have instructed, master."

When the immortal left, Khiann took the chair he had vacated and put his elbows on his knees. "I wanted to ask if you've made progress with the matter we have discussed before."

Navohn smiled, then cast a soundproofing shroud around his office. "Yes, I did. It will cost me a great fortune, but then the happiness of my only son is worth it." He winked. "As is the future of our people."

Khiann closed his eyes and took his first deep breath in two days. "Care to share it with me?"

Navohn reached under the table and lifted a sealed pitcher of beer. "Bring two cups from the cupboard over there." He pointed.

When Khiann did as instructed, Navohn broke the seal on the pitcher and poured the brew into the two cups. "This is one of the best of Ninkasi's brews."

"Does she still send you free samples?"

"It is not really free. She is interested in exporting and wants me to help her promote her beers. I am taking quite a few barrels with me on this expedition."

"It is good business. Instead of going empty and returning with merchandise, you trade both ways."

"That is the idea." He pointed at Khiann's cup. "What do you think?"

He took a sip. "It is very good. But then I like all of Ninkasi's beers."

"It is excellent. I hope to make a good profit selling it." He winked. "It will pay for some of the goods I have to part with to gain Ahn's ear."

Khiann took another big gulp, then put the empty cup on the table. "So that is how you plan to do it? Dazzle Ahn with gifts?"

Navohn shrugged. "It's always worked before. I asked for an audience with Ahn this evening under the pretext of discussing the armed escort he had promised me. I will bring extravagant gifts as a show of gratitude for his help. And while we go back and forth, with him declining politely and me insisting on him accepting the gifts, I will broach the subject of the princess's infatuation with you, and yours with her, and see how he reacts."

His father was a master negotiator. If anyone could pull it off, it was he. "I wish I could come with you and see you working your magic."

"I wish you could. But this conversation is best done between us, the two fathers."

"How are you going to accomplish a private meeting with Ahn? From what you have told me, Nai always sits with her mate, and as of late so does Annani."

"Not on the third day of the week, which happens to be today." Navohn smirked. "That is when Nai has her own meetings with the palace staff, and I think it is safe to assume that Annani is required to attend with her mother."

4

ANNANI

"That was so clever of Khiann," Annani sighed. "Can you go and get your sister?"

Gulan, who a moment ago looked flustered after talking with Esag, switched modes from excited to worried. "This is not a good idea, my lady," she whispered. "Are you going to wear Tula's clothes again and sneak into the gardens to see Master Khiann? What if someone sees you kissing him while you are shrouding yourself in Tula's image? Imagine the scandal." The maid's chest was heaving as she worked herself up into a frenzy. "Master Khiann can get into a lot of trouble for that. Tula is just a little girl. And what would people think of her?"

"Relax, Gulan. Everything will be all right. Tell Esag that Master Khiann can come over later this evening to talk with Tula who indeed needs more help with her school project. Also, tell him that you are very grateful for his master's generous offer of help."

Gulan groaned. "As you wish, my lady." She bowed obediently.

As her friend left the room, Annani allowed herself to drop the confident expression she had worn for Gulan's benefit.

The truth was that she was nervous.

For some reason, seeing Khiann again filled her with trepidation. It was strange that when she had snuck out to see him, there had been none of that. There had been no second-guessing her decision, no hesitation.

Thinking back, Annani realized that it had taken courage to proposition a god. And yet, she had thought nothing of it.

But now that she was going to see Khiann again, the insecurities that had been absent before were manifesting. Perhaps she was better at action than inaction, better at initiating than awaiting another's move.

Wiping her sweaty palms on the skirt of her dress, Annani walked over to the mirror and examined her reflection, trying to see herself through Khiann's eyes.

What did he find desirable about her?

She cupped her small breasts and sighed, wishing she had large ones like Gulan's. Males liked curves. Big-breasted females with flaring hips were considered desirable, while skinny short maidens not so much.

Her face was beautiful, everyone said so, but was it enough to inspire lust in a grown man?

Khiann had gotten hard while kissing her, but maybe it was an instinctive response, and maybe he would have reacted the same to any female sitting in his lap?

Two days ago she had set out to seduce Khiann with

her usual confidence and the belief that she was the most beautiful of goddesses. Her mission had been successful, and she had returned to the palace happy and confident.

What had changed?

Why the sudden doubts?

The answer had been lurking in the back of her mind all along, but she had refused to acknowledge it until now.

Khiann had required more convincing than she had expected.

He had not fallen to his knees, grateful for her interest in him and her offer. That was the source of the unfamiliar insecurities and doubts.

Winning the argument and convincing him to pursue her had felt like a victory at first, but later, when she had time to think and go over every word that had been uttered between them, Annani's heart had lost some of its buoyancy.

She should have known better than to expect unbridled passion and a declaration of eternal devotion. After all, Khiann had been successful in pretending not to notice her for years. And yet, in her secret maidenly fantasies, she had hoped he would not need any convincing whatsoever.

She had hoped he would be so taken with her that he would be willing to sacrifice everything and go to war for her.

Silly girl that she was.

An inexperienced virgin who knew nothing of seduction.

But she was not stupid, and she could no longer

repress the seeds of doubt that had sprouted in her heart. Too much was at stake to keep hiding the truth from herself.

If Khiann did not find her irresistible, then he was not her truelove mate. A male god was supposed to be lustful and demanding, especially with his destined one and only.

And yet Khiann had ignored her for years, which should have been impossible for him even if he had been only pretending. That was not how it worked between fated couples.

Annani closed her eyes and took several calming breaths.

It went against her impetuous nature, but this time Annani was going to remain passive and let him do all the work. She was not going to initiate a thing. It was Khiann's turn to take a risk and bare his soul to her. If he was not willing, then he was not the one for her.

It would break her heart, but it was better to discover the truth before she risked her father's displeasure and incited Mortdh to war for nothing.

"My lady?" Gulan entered her room. "Tula is here. Should I have her come in?"

Annani schooled her features and smiled broadly. "Of course."

The little girl, who was a much braver soul than her older sister, practically skipped into the room. "I am so excited. Are we going to play the game again?"

Annani put a finger to her lips. "Shush, keep your voice down."

Tula giggled. "I am sorry, my lady," she whispered loudly. "How are we going to do it this time?"

How indeed.

Instead of coming up with a plan, Annani had wasted her time on the most ineffective activity possible.

Self-doubt was a human affliction, not one that should affect powerful goddesses, and certainly not the future leader of the realm. She was inexperienced, that was true, but she was young and therefore entitled to a few mistakes. As Ekin had always told her, it was better to try and fail than not try at all. Failing was part of the learning process.

When all was said and done, Annani would persevere because she was not a quitter. She was a fighter, and she was a winner.

Beckoning for Tula to get closer, she whispered, "The same way we did it last time. We switch clothes, and you get in my bed."

"I love your bed. It is so comfortable. I feel like a princess when I am in it." The girl frowned. "I wanted to ask you a question, but Gulan said I should not, but I want to ask anyway. If you can shroud yourself in my visage, why do you need to wear my clothes?"

Gulan paled. "Tula, this is rude. Apologize immediately!"

Annani waved a hand. "It is okay, Gulan." She smiled at the girl. "How good is your thralling ability? Can you shroud yourself from humans?"

Tula grimaced. "Not good at all. I can hold a shroud for a couple of minutes, but I lose concentration if someone talks to me, and my shroud goes poof!"

Funny girl.

Annani leaned closer. "I can hold a shroud for a little

longer than you, and I can even have a conversation while keeping it around me, but it requires a lot of effort, and I cannot hold on to it for long. This is why I need the disguise."

Tula seemed taken aback. "I thought gods could do it for as long as they want." She made a face. "I even thought that maybe gods are not really as perfect and as beautiful as they seem and that they only shroud themselves to look so flawless."

Gulan gasped. "Tula! This is most disrespectful. Apologize at once!"

"What?" The girl spread her arms. "Am I not allowed to think? Or am I just not allowed to talk?'

Annani patted the girl's bony shoulder. "It is okay to think, but sometimes it is better to keep your thoughts to yourself. I am not offended, but some other gods might be. It is always better to err on the side of caution."

Gulan tried to stifle a snort as she led Tula behind the partition, but it escaped her throat. She covered it up with a quick command to her sister; "Take your tunic off, Tula."

The older girl was smart and cautious. But what was the fun in that?

"Your sister would like me to follow my own advice, which I do not always do, but that does not mean that it is not good."

"My lady." Gulan's eyes darted to Annani's wardrobe. "May I just make a suggestion?"

Annani waved a hand. "Certainly. You should always feel free to express your opinion."

Her maid came closer and whispered in her ear.

"Instead of meeting Master Khiann once again dressed in Tula's unflattering commoner garb, perhaps this time you would like to impress him by wearing one of your own beautiful dresses? You can come with the two of us, claiming that you want to listen in on Master Khiann's talk with Tula because you want to learn about commerce. No one is going to question your desire to do so. On the contrary, your sire might commend your interest in the subject."

Hmm, that was an angle Annani had not considered. A nice dress would bolster her confidence and would make her much harder to resist.

It would also be easier to act regal and aloof when dressed like a princess who had reached her majority, and not a young commoner girl.

5

AHN

"Navohn, my friend, what brings you here this evening?" Ahn asked.

Earlier that day, a messenger had arrived from the merchant, requesting a meeting. The stated reason was Navohn's desire to discuss the escort Ahn had promised him, but since there was nothing to discuss, it was probably about something else. As far as Ahn was concerned, he had done his part, and the rest should have been handled by underlings.

Nevertheless, Navohn was good company, and he was looking forward to an informal chat with his old friend. The god was an excellent source of reliable information that otherwise would have never made its way to the palace.

As a ruler, Ahn had no direct connection with his people—gods, immortals, and humans—and was dependent on reports prepared by others, whose alliances and loyalties he did not always trust. He would have been a fool to do so.

Most people, regardless of species, were motivated either by fear or by greed. It was a rare individual who was concerned with the greater good.

Navohn was a good male, but Ahn had no illusions as to his motives being purely altruistic. Ahn's long-standing friendship benefited the merchant and his family, ensuring that their status remained high despite his friend's odd choice of occupation.

Also, supplying the palace was a most profitable business.

That being said, however, at his core Navohn was a truly decent fellow, who believed that the system the gods had developed to govern themselves and those they ruled over was as just and as fair as anything anyone could come up with and needed to be preserved.

They had that belief in common.

Navohn bowed deeply. "I knew I would have your ear alone this evening while your lady is busy elsewhere, my lord." He pulled a small wrapped package from a pocket hidden between the folds of his robe.

Ahn beckoned him to come closer. "Come, sit with me." He offered Navohn the chair across from him.

"You honor me, my lord." The merchant climbed the two steps up the dais, bowed again, and then took the seat he had been offered.

With a wave of his hand, Ahn dismissed his secretary and his guards, so he and Navohn could drop the formalities and talk like the old friends they were. Other than Nai, the merchant was the only one Ahn could have a normal conversation with.

Navohn waited for everyone to depart before placing the package on the low table between the two chairs. "The anniversary of your joining ceremony with your beautiful mate is coming up, and I knew you would need a special gift for her."

Ahn smiled. "What would I have done without you, my friend? Your excellent memory ensures my mated bliss. Once again I had forgotten."

"My memory is far from excellent. I keep a calendar of special occasions—mine as well as those of my close friends."

"It is much appreciated. Show me what you have in that parcel. By the size of it, I am guessing jewelry?"

"What else?"

Navohn untied the twine, then proceeded to unwrap his package slowly and carefully, probably not out of concern for the fragility of what was inside, but to build up anticipation. After all, he was a merchant who knew how to enhance the perceived value of his wares.

When he was done, Navohn arranged the set for Ahn's inspection.

Made of gold and studded with glowing red stones the likes of which Ahn had never seen before, the necklace was an intricate work of expert craftsmanship that must have taken many moon cycles to create. There was only one artisan who could have produced it, and he was not cheap. Navohn must have paid a fortune to have it made. A matching set of earrings and two bracelets completed the exquisite ensemble.

"Lady Nai will be most pleased when you present her with this gift."

"I am sure she will." Ahn lifted the necklace. "Beautiful stones. I have never seen such vivid red. Where did you get this?"

"Down south of the Nile river. I have never seen the likes either. They came at a steep price, but I knew the stones would look magnificent once Master Khirin set them in gold."

"I recognize his work. It is incomparable." The master goldsmith was a true artisan who took insane pride in his work. Each piece took many moon cycles to complete, and he charged for his work accordingly.

"When did you commission this set?"

Navohn leaned back in his chair and steepled his fingers. "A year ago, right after I returned from the trip to the south. I knew right away that these stones would look magnificent on your beautiful mate, and that lady Nai would appreciate having something so unique."

"Indeed." Ahn put the necklace back. "What is your price for these?" He waved his hand over the set.

The merchant bowed his head. "It is a gift. After all, you refused payment for the armed escort you are providing for my upcoming expedition."

Ahn frowned. The escort was in exchange for information he wanted Navohn to gather and bring back to him. It had never been stated in so many words, but it had been implied and understood. Navohn had something else in mind as payment for the extravagant gift.

"It is not a fair exchange. The escort is not worth even a tenth of the value of this set." Ahn pushed the parcel toward Navohn, not because he did not want the gift, but because it was part of the game they were playing.

The merchant pushed the parcel back. "I cannot put a price on true love, my friend. Your fated mate deserves only the best."

"Indeed she does. But I have the means to pay for my mate's joining anniversary gift." He pushed the parcel toward Navohn again. "Name your price."

The merchant sighed dramatically and spread his arms. "What price would you have me put on love, my lord?"

Insufferable god. What did he want?

"As much as I appreciate our friendship, Navohn, I do not appreciate talking in circles. Tell me what you want."

The sparkle in the guy's eyes was a sure sign that he had Ahn exactly where he wanted him, but at this point, Ahn did not care. His curiosity had been whetted.

"True love needs to be celebrated and revered and nothing should supersede it. Not politics, not monetary concerns, not even pride. Do you agree, my lord?"

Ahn did not like where this was going. That much preamble meant a grand request was coming.

"To an extent. Not everyone is fortunate enough to find their truelove mate or even have the luxury of seeking one."

"But you are one of those fortunate to have found yours."

Ahn inclined his head. "And I thank the Fates every day for the blessing they bestowed on me."

Navohn nodded. "As you should, my lord, as you should." He shook his head and spread his arms again. "Do you not think that your daughter deserves the same?"

The words were like a kick to the gut, especially when delivered by a friend.

The guilt over the promise Ahn had made Mortdh

was a source of endless torment, and yet he saw no way out of it. To break it was akin to a declaration of war. The offense to Mortdh would be too great, and it would push him over the edge.

Even a sane god would have taken that as the worst insult possible. And Mortdh was far from sane.

Ahn threw a quick soundproofing shroud over the room before responding. He was well aware that Mortdh had spies even in the heart of the palace. "You overstep your bounds, my friend. My daughter is the future ruler of this realm. It is her duty to ensure peace."

Navohn sighed. "It will be many years before her time comes to take the throne, and a lot can happen between now and then. Peace is not guaranteed either way."

"Perhaps not. But let us face the facts instead of engaging in wishful thinking. Breaking Annani's engagement to Mortdh will bring about immediate war. It will be perceived as a grave offense, and he would have no choice but to respond even if he is not so inclined, which we both know he is."

Navohn lifted a finger. "Unless it is not you who breaks the engagement, but the lady herself. If Annani finds her truelove match, she has the right to choose her beloved over the one she is promised to. It is our law that matings must be consensual, and naturally, after finding her fated one, the lady cannot consent to join another. The dissolving of an engagement is not considered an offense in such a case. On the contrary. Truelove matings are regarded as decreed by the Fates. To go against them is considered sacrilege."

It was a loophole Ahn had contemplated before.

For it to work, though, Annani would need to find her truelove match, which was not likely. He had even entertained the thought of arranging a ruse. But to prevent war, it had to be proven beyond a shadow of a doubt that her chosen mate was indeed her one and only—not easy to do even when true.

Ahn rubbed a hand over his jaw. "As powerful as I am, even I cannot force the Fates to provide a truelove mate for my daughter."

Navohn smiled. "Perhaps the Fates have already sent him to her?"

Ahn lifted a brow. "Do you know something I do not?"

The merchant bowed his head. "Indeed, I do, my lord. Your daughter and my son seem to be under the impression that they might be each other's one and only. They would like your permission to explore the possibility."

6

KHIANN

As Khiann waited for Annani in the palace's gardens, he wondered how their second meeting was going to play out. He might have set things in motion, but the rest was in Annani's hands.

Would she come alone as Tula?

Or would Gulan accompany her?

Or perhaps Annani would come as herself, using some excuse for why she needed to be with the girls?

The problem with the third option was that her guards would trail along. Gulan and Tula were participants in his and Annani's conspiracy. Willingly or not, they would cooperate, giving them privacy.

The guards were a different story.

He could thrall the immortals with ease, but they might suspect him of doing so. Khiann could not risk that. If he hoped to ever get Ahn's permission to court Annani, he had to be on his best behavior.

Which probably meant no kisses.

Then again, maybe Annani could thrall her guards.

After all, she had done so before. Ahn let his daughter get away with a lot of escapades, and she would most likely not get in any trouble for a small offense like that—or as small as she would make it seem.

Khiann's plans for her did not fall under the category of insignificant transgressions.

Hopefully, she was just as desperate for more as he.

More kisses, more touching. Khiann wanted his hands all over her slender body, caressing, coaxing, exciting...

She would not object.

The little minx was lustful and ripe for the taking.

Annani needed him as much as he needed her.

What in damnation was taking her so long?

He pushed to his feet and started pacing. It was early evening, which was the time gods and immortals usually began venturing outside their darkened, cool abodes, while the humans did the reverse, retiring for the night.

A small exodus was happening in the gardens, the caretakers passing him by on their way out, casting curious glances at the god who was not supposed to be there. As they bowed deeply to show their respect, Khiann nodded graciously and uttered a few words of blessing.

Humans expected that from gods. In exchange for the gods' teachings and blessings, many provided their labor free of charge. Those working in the palace were not worshipers and were paid good wages, but still, it was customary.

As the sound of girly giggles preceded his visitors, Khiann turned in their direction, waiting for the three to emerge through the gate. The amused voices belonged to Annani and Tula. Gulan looked terrified. Not that his gaze lingered on the maid's worried face for more than a split second before moving to the magnificent princess and getting stuck there.

It seemed Annani had chosen the third option, looking resplendent in her regal attire and her jewelry, with her abundant red hair spilling in soft locks down her back and reaching all the way down to her thighs.

Wiping a hand over his mouth, Khiann commanded his fangs to behave. Unfortunately, he could do nothing about the other part of his male anatomy that was showing signs of excitement. Hoping that his long tunic with its gold-thread embroidery would provide some coverage, he bowed deeply.

"My lady, I am honored that you would join us for the lesson. I did not know you were interested in commerce." His words were for the benefit of the two guards trailing behind the girls.

There would be no privacy for them today.

Annani lifted her chin and clasped her hands in front of her. "I am interested in everything that has to do with the prosperity of my people. As a future ruler, it is my obligation to learn as much as I can about as many things as I can."

He bowed again. "You are very wise."

Gulan sighed, Tula giggled again, and Annani smirked.

Turning to face her maid, she pointed at one of the trails. "I know the perfect place for today's lesson. You know the one I am referring to—the gazebo next to the fountain with my mother's statue in the middle."

"Yes, my lady." Gulan dipped her head, took Tula's hand, and proceeded in the direction the princess had indicated.

Annani and Khiann followed with the guards closing the procession.

"How have you been lately, my lady?" Khiann asked.

"Very well. Thank you for asking. And yourself?"

"I have been perturbed. Sleep eluded me and I was restless."

She arched a red brow. "What troubles you?"

"My father's expedition. There are many dangers on the road. I hope the most wise Ahn will provide a large armed escort for the caravan. In fact, my father is meeting with him as we speak."

As Annani's quick mind caught up to his meaning immediately, her breath hitched a little before she could control the response. "I wish your father much success and a safe journey. I hope my father will do right by him."

Waterfall sounds greeted them as they neared the fountain, the gazebo with its stone table and two stone benches coming into view. Annani was right. It was the perfect spot for conducting a lesson, but not so much for the other things Khiann had in mind.

How in damnation was he going to steal a kiss?

Khiann refused to even contemplate returning home without one.

Annani took a seat on the bench next to the stone table and motioned for him to join her. "Gulan, Tula, you can sit on the other bench."

After the girls had done as she'd instructed, Annani turned to the guards who had remained standing outside. “Please go to the kitchen and bring us refreshments. Tell cook to bake the sweet cakes I love. When they are ready, bring them here together with a pitcher of beer and another one of water.”

To ensure the guards' cooperation, her words had been infused with the gentlest of thralls. It had been so subtle that he was sure none of the immortals perceived it. This was not the work of a novice. Annani must have been practicing long and hard to get such a level of mastery. In fact, she was better at it than he was.

Gulan frowned, probably suspecting something, but that was because she knew her lady well and not because she had felt something. Khiann was certain of that.

Tula pulled out a clay tablet and a stylus from her satchel. “Should we pretend to actually do some studying?”

Annani waved a hand. “How silly of me. I forgot to ask the men to bring a tablecloth. Could you girls bring one? Napkins too. And a vase with flowers. After all, we cannot enjoy a repast on an unadorned table, can we?”

This time Annani had not used a thrall. There was no need. Her co-conspirators were going to obey her wishes.

Gulan sighed. “Come on, Tula. Let us get what the lady asks for.”

The little girl giggled. “I will spend the next hour looking for the most beautiful flowers in the garden for your vase, my lady.”

Khiann liked the girl, a lot. “Remind me to buy the sprite a gift,” he said after the girls had departed.

"Tula is a good sport. Poor Gulan, though. She trembles in fear every time I pull a stunt like this."

He scooted a little closer and wrapped his arm around Annani's shoulders. "I hope that by a stunt like this you are not referring to arranging clandestine meetings with other male gods."

Annani leaned away, putting some distance between them before casting a silencing shroud around the gazebo. "It depends. Are you asking about the past or the future?"

It was difficult to shroud a space without walls, and Khiann could feel the ripples as outside sounds filtered through. He wondered whether he should reinforce it with one of his own. Annani might take offense, but it was important to keep their conversation private for several reasons, chief among them the possibility of Mortdh having spies inside the palace.

As Khiann cast the shroud, the bubble he incased them in snapped into place with an audible pop. "Both," he said, his words sounding as if he was talking inside a sealed chamber, which he kind of was. Now there were two shrouds protecting their privacy. Annani's was the outer layer, and his was the inner one.

Double security.

The princess did not remark on it, although she was clearly aware of what he had done. Hopefully, it meant that she approved.

Instead, Annani touched a small finger to her luscious lips. "Hmm, let me think." She tapped her lips twice. "I have only done this once, two days ago. The meeting this evening was your idea, not mine. But I cannot say about the future. That depends on you and your actions or lack thereof."

What did she mean?

He was doing everything in his power to move forward and get his courtship approved by Ahn. Or rather his father was doing it for him.

"Right now my father is talking with yours, and we will soon know if there is a chance Ahn will approve of my request to court you."

Annani sighed. "That is between my father and yours, and it is out of our hands. What about what is or is not between the two of us?"

Baffling woman.

Why was she speaking in riddles?

Was it a test of some sort?

Khiann considered himself an intelligent god. He should be able to figure it out. Had he inadvertently offended Annani in some way?

A moment of strained silence passed as he searched his mind and came up with nothing. "Please forgive me, but I do not know what you mean. You will have to be more direct."

Annani sighed. "I really hoped you would act differently once we were alone. I cannot help but feel disappointed."

7

ANNANI

Are all males so obtuse?

Except, it did not matter if Khiann understood her meaning or not. His action, or rather inaction, spoke louder than words.

If he desired her even a fraction of how much she desired him, he would have been ravishing her the moment she had gotten rid of her guards and had sent Gulan and Tula away.

Even though Annani had promised herself to remain passive this evening and let Khiann lead, she had taken the first step by inviting him to sit next to her on the bench. It was a clear signal that she was not only allowing his advances but inviting them.

All he had to do was reach over, pull her into his lap, and start kissing. But had he?

No.

Instead, he was wasting valuable time talking.

"What would you have me do?" Khiann asked.

Shaking her head, Annani pushed up to her feet. "If I have to tell you then you are not the right god for me."

"Oh no, you do not." Khiann grabbed her by the wrist and pulled her back down so forcefully that she fell into his lap.

"What are you doing?" Annani asked a little breathlessly. This was exactly what she had wanted him to do, but for the right reasons. Not because he had gotten angry or offended by her dismissal.

"I came here for another kiss, and I am not leaving before I get one."

Reaching under her hair, his hand closed around her nape. His fingers were so long that he was practically encircling her entire throat, but he was gentle, caging her neck but not hurting her in any way. And as his lips descended upon hers, he stopped right before contact was made, waiting for her to close the remaining distance.

Even in the height of passion, Khiann remembered to seek her consent, which was the way it should be. A male, even a dominant god, should always ensure that his advances were welcome. It did not detract one bit from the intensity Annani sought. On the contrary, it added to it.

With a sigh that sounded more like a moan, Annani pressed her lips to Khiann's, and by doing so snapped his restraint as surely as if she had severed the tether holding a wild animal.

With her permission explicitly granted, Khiann's ferocity was unleashed.

And she had thought he did not desire her.

Not only could she not have been more wrong,

Annani had never been happier about having been mistaken.

As he devoured her with his lips and his tongue, his hands roamed her back impatiently, urgently, the circles growing nearer and nearer the sides of her breasts.

When was he going to touch her there?

Her nipples hardening into two aching points, she moaned into Khiann's mouth and pressed her breasts to his hard chest.

"Is that what you want, little girl?" he hissed from in between his elongated fangs.

It was a testament to how much she was turned on that his comment did not bother her. Khiann could call her a little girl, or whatever else he wanted, as long as he kept touching her.

"Yes. More," she mumbled into his mouth, slipping her own tongue inside and tasting his exquisite male flavor. The effect was like getting drunk. She felt dizzy and lightheaded.

And happy.

So incredibly happy that she could burst from how much happiness was inside her.

Annani could never get enough of this. As soon as her father granted Khiann permission to court her, she was going to take this magnificent male to her bed. Or his. Or whatever bed was available.

Perhaps even before permission was given.

Every moment that they were not joined was a wasted one, and it did not matter that they had eternity ahead of them to enjoy each other.

His hand brushed against the side of her breast,

dangerously close to her nipple, and then halted. "More?" he asked.

"Yes. More, more, and more."

When he palmed her through the dress, they both groaned in unison.

As Annani felt herself grow wet and needy between her legs, she knew what it meant. Her mother had had the talk with her in that matter-of-fact way of hers, which had failed to mention how incredible the sensations were.

It was so much more than Annani had anticipated.

The pleasure was intense, but there was also the ache of an unfulfilled void. She knew what it meant as well. In theory.

"Is that good?" Khiann whispered in her ear.

"It is. But I ache for more."

"Impatient girl." He nipped her soft earlobe, the small sting ratcheting her desire to a new level.

Who knew a little pain could enhance pleasure?

The body was indeed a marvelous thing.

"Do it again," she said, wanting to make sure she had not confused the sensation.

"Did you like it?" He licked her earlobe instead, sending shivers down her spine.

"I did. But I do not understand why."

His fingers closed around her nipple, and as he pinched it lightly, her eyes rolled back, and more moisture gathered down below.

"Did you like this?"

"Yes," she whispered.

He palmed her breast, warming her nipple, and kissed her again, his lips soft this time, patient.

"There is so much I can teach you, my beautiful flower."

The words excited and upset her at the same time. Excited, because she was eager to discover all the wonders of intimacy. Upset, because it reminded her that Khiann had sampled plenty of other females before her.

"Promise me that you will never bed another female. You belong to me."

He chuckled. "From the moment you kissed me, I could think of no one but you. There will never be another. If your father refuses my suit, I shall take a vow of celibacy."

Annani rested her forehead on Khiann's chest. "No, I would not want that for you. If we cannot be together, I want you to find another." She smiled sadly. "Just make sure it is no one I know. And never bring her to the palace. At least not for a few years."

He sighed. "You are pure heart, Annani."

She lifted her head. "Did you hear that?"

Khiann listened for a moment and then smiled. "Now I do. I think Tula is singing to let us know that they are coming back." His hand closed around her nape again. "One last kiss."

"Yes, please."

8

KHIANN

Khiann joined his parents in the carriage for the trip to the palace, instead of riding his horse behind it. As much as he loved the stallion, he did not want to arrive with the animal's scent all over him, or with his tunic in less than pristine condition.

Today's audience with Ahn and Nai was the most important of his life.

"You have nothing to worry about," his father said.

"What if Ahn does not approve of me?"

Navohn waved a hand, casting a sound barrier to keep their conversation private. "This is only a formality. What is not to approve of? You are a fine young god who any parent would be happy to secure for his or her daughter."

Contrary to his father's reassurances, Khiann's age was a problem. At nineteen, he did not inspire the same respect as an older, more experienced god would. "I am too young. Ahn might want a mature mate for Annani, someone who will help her and guide her in case she has to assume rule sooner than expected."

His mother laughed. "What on earth could happen that would require the princess to do so? She has thousands of years ahead of her to learn all she needs to know, and so do you. When the time comes, both of you are going to be well prepared."

Navohn patted Khiann's shoulder. "As I said before. Unless you mumble like a fool, it is a done deal. Ahn wants Annani to be happy, but he does not want war with Mortdh. Therefore, your courtship would have to be done in secret. Once she announces you as her truelove mate, Mortdh would be bound by tradition to bow out gracefully. He will not lose face, and war would be averted."

Crossing his arms over his chest, Khiann leaned back against the plush pillows lining the carriage's back and sides. What did a secret courtship involve?

And how exactly were they going to keep it a secret?

The palace was teeming with numerous immortals and humans who held various positions, and no doubt included quite a few who spied for Mortdh.

Was he going to sneak into Annani's room under a shroud?

Should he think of a solution or wait for Ahn to suggest one?

But the most important question was whether Annani was going to attend this meeting.

It would be hard to concentrate with her present. For the past two days, Khiann could think of nothing else but the few intimate moments they had stolen in the gardens.

As the carriage stopped in front of the palace's gates, servants rushed to attend to them and their entourage.

The doors to the palace were open, with Ahn's personal secretary standing just outside them and waiting to welcome Khiann's parents, which reflected Navohn's high standing with the ruler.

"Greetings," he said as he bowed deep to the elder gods and only inclined his head toward Khiann. "Lord Ahn is expecting you. Please follow me." The immortal led Khiann and his parents into a small reception hall. "Please be seated." He motioned to one of the two long divans flanking a low stone table.

As the three of them waited in silence, it took Khiann a few moments to realize what bothered him about the setup that was otherwise welcoming and not as intimidating as the throne room. With no burning incense to corrupt the air, the chamber was not stifling.

Which meant that there would be no hiding their emotions from the ruler and his mate. It was a well-known fact that Ahn could detect the tiniest variations in scent, and that it was impossible to hide things from him.

By the same token, Ahn and Nai would be similarly exposed. The difference was that neither Khiann's nor his parents' senses were as sharp as Ahn's, and that put them at a disadvantage.

But this was not about Ahn or Khiann's parents. This was about Khiann.

He was here to be tested, which was perfectly fine with him.

He was ready.

His intentions toward Annani were pure. Well, aside

from a burning need to bed her, but then it was expected of him. A lack of intense desire for the one he wanted to court would have probably disqualified him.

Gods were lustful creatures, especially toward their trueloves.

A few moments later, when one of the doors opened, Khiann's gut twisted in anticipation. But instead of Annani and her parents, a flurry of servants entered, holding trays loaded with refreshments.

A long time passed until the doors were opened again by two guards, who bowed deeply as Ahn strode in with Nai at his side. Annani walked a couple of steps behind them.

Khiann and his parents got to their feet and bowed, staying in the position until Ahn and Nai sat down at the divan across from them. When Annani sat next to her mother, Ahn motioned for her to move in between them.

"Please sit down, my friends," Ahn said. "This is an informal occasion. Make yourselves comfortable."

With a wave of his hand, their ruler dismissed the servants and the two guards, who bowed and retreated, walking backward until they cleared the room.

As the doors clicked closed, Nai motioned at the table. "Please partake."

Khiann glanced at Annani, but she shook her head imperceptibly, letting him know he should focus on her father.

Smart girl. He would do well to follow her instructions.

"Thank you, my lady," Navohn said. "And thank you for agreeing to see us, my lord."

Ahn waved his hand again, casting a soundproofing shroud around the chamber. Their ruler's power was immense, his shroud snapping into place and sealing them inside an impenetrable shield. Compared to this, the one Navohn had cast in the carriage seemed like a child's practice attempt.

"Khiann." Ahn pinned him with a hard stare. "Your father tells me that you and my daughter have exchanged messages, deciding that you are each other's destined mates."

To protect Annani, that was how his father had explained it. But to continue the lie without the benefit of incense to mask their scents would be foolish. Besides, Annani might have confessed already.

Khiann bowed his head. "We exchanged words, my lord."

Ahn nodded, the small smile curving one side of his mouth making him look cruel. "I see. What I want to know is who snuck to see whom?" He cast an inquiring glance at Annani.

Not one to cower before anyone, not even the formidable Ahn, Annani lifted her chin. "I snuck out first to see Khiann, and then he came to the palace under the pretext of meeting Tula, Gulan's little sister, and helping her with her school project."

"I assume Tula had no such assignment?" Still looking amused, which was a good sign, Ahn lifted a brow.

Annani shook her head. "No."

"And how did you manage to elude your guards and sneak out to see Khiann?"

She rolled her eyes. "Oh please, Father, as if it was

difficult. I ordered Tula to get in my bed and pretend she was me, and then shrouded myself in her image. The guards thought that the two girls leaving my room were Gulan and her sister, and that I was sleeping in my chambers."

"So you forced both Gulan and Tula into being your accomplices?"

"I did. Please do not be mad at them. I gave them no choice. And Khiann did not know what I was planning to do either. But I had to talk to him and convince him to come ask your permission to court me."

Nai was shaking her head while hiding a smile, and Ahn seemed to have trouble keeping a stern expression as well. It was obvious the two adored their daughter.

"What kind of project was Tula supposed to work on?" Ahn asked.

Annani lifted her hand and waved at Khiann. "Commerce, of course. That is why she needed Khiann's help."

"I see." He rubbed a hand over his square jaw. "This gives me an idea for a punishment. One that fits your crime."

Annani's eyes widened in surprise. "Punishment? Is your displeasure with me not enough?"

"Not this time, daughter. You put yourself in danger, and you coerced your poor maid into endangering her little sister."

Khiann would have been worried for Annani if not for Ahn's smirk. A quick glance at Nai revealed her hiding a smile with a hand over her mouth, but her eyes betrayed her, sparkling with amusement.

Ahn leveled his gaze at Khiann. "And you, my friend's son. What do you have to say for yourself?"

Khiann bowed his head. "I cannot apologize, my lord, since my apology would not be sincere. I have adored Annani since we were children in school, but I have never entertained even the tiniest of hopes that she might be my fated truelove. I did not dare. But when she came to see me, I was grateful and elated, thanking the Fates for her courage and castigating myself for not acting first. I am humbled by Annani's determination and her will to act upon it. She will make a fine ruler one day."

Seeming pleased by Khiann's sincere answer, Ahn nodded. "You have guts, Khiann. If you were a coward who trembled in fear before me, I would have declined your suit. Not only because my Annani needs a strong mate to stand up to her, but because she needs you to lend her your strength and support. My daughter's journey is not going to be easy. It is going to be fraught with peril."

Khiann bowed his head again. "It would be my honor and my privilege."

"That being said, you were a co-conspirator in Annani's scheme and therefore will share in her punishment."

"Of course, my lord." As long as his suit was accepted, Khiann was willing to suffer any torment Ahn could come up with.

Except, Annani joining him in the punishment was not going to happen. If Ahn needed to punish someone, he could do as he pleased with Khiann, but not Annani. He was about to speak up when she beat him to it.

"What punishment, Father?" Annani asked in a tone that was defiant and not at all fearful.

"I appoint Khiann as your tutor. That project Tula supposedly had to do for school is now yours. You are to prepare a full and detailed report on the subject of commerce. Khiann is going to come to the palace every day after his work for his father is done and teach you what he knows. You are to compile this knowledge into a comprehensive report and submit it to me in one moon rotation."

As Annani realized her father's plan, a smile spread across her beautiful face. "Does this mean that the old goat is no longer my tutor and Khiann is taking his place?"

"For one moon rotation. After that time I will reevaluate, depending on the quality of that report." Ahn winked. "And, of course, on the level of dedication the two of you show."

9

AHN

"I like the boy," Nai said as they retired to their bedchamber for the night. "He is handsome."

Ahn arched a brow. "Is that the only criterion for a suitable mate for your daughter? All gods are handsome, and all goddesses are beautiful."

"I am not referring to his features, although they are most pleasing, it is his bearing that impresses me." Nai sat on the bed and removed her sandals. "He is confident without being arrogant, and he is honest without being foolish about it. Besides, did you see how Annani looked at him?"

Ahn sat next to his mate and wrapped his arm around her. "It is the same look you gave me when I first saw you bathing in that pond. It got me in a lot of trouble."

"Are you sorry that I entrapped you?"

He kissed the top of her head. "How many times have you asked me this question, and how many times have I answered never?"

She laughed. "Thousands."

None other than he got to see this side of his mate. Mindful of her humble beginnings, Nai always strove to appear regal and composed. She only dropped that mask when they were alone. It was in moments like these, with her face relaxed and her laughter free and uninhibited, that he loved her the most.

"I thank the Fates every day for your incredible courage to do what you did. If not for your subterfuge, I would have been mated to my cousin, and she would have made my life miserable. Instead, you forced my hand and made me the happiest of gods."

She leaned her head on his shoulder. "You were mine, I knew it the moment I saw you. I could not wait until I was of mating age because it would have been too late, and you would have mated your intended." Even after all these years, and all of his reassurances, Nai still felt the need to explain herself and why she had acted the way she had. Others might have scorned her, even to this day, but not him. Nevertheless, Ahn liked to tease her about it.

"So it had nothing to do with my status?"

Nai huffed. "You have asked me that same question thousands of times, and my answer has always been the same." She mimicked his words to her. "No. I would have done the same if you were the lowliest of gods. You are my truelove. I have a feeling Annani and Khiann are the real deal too. I hope so, for her sake. It always saddened me to think of her in a loveless joining with Mortdh. He would have squashed her spirit."

"I hope I am not committing a grave mistake." Ahn sighed. "Even though bowing out would be the right thing to do, when Mortdh finds out, he will be enraged nonetheless. Fates only know what he will do."

"You can offer him Areana as consolation. She is second in line after Annani."

"He will not accept a much older daughter from a mistress, especially not one who was already mated."

Areana was Ahn's only other child. Born a century before Nai had entered his life, she was older than his mate, who had been only sixteen when he had joined with her.

The pledge of eternal fidelity Ahn had made for taking Nai a year shy of her majority had turned out to be superfluous. Since their first fateful encounter, he had never desired anyone but her.

"Widowed," Nai shook her head. "The poor woman. It has been years since her mate was killed, and yet she still mourns him and refuses to consider another."

"Bandits are the bane of our existence. I wish there were more of us to eliminate this plague once and for all."

"You could do what Mortdh is doing and assemble an army of humans to fight them. He is insane but not stupid."

Ahn shook his head. "I will not stoop that low. Humans serve and worship us in exchange for our benevolent leadership and guidance. I will not repay their trust by leading them into a war that will result in countless casualties. Our obligation is to help them live good lives. Sacrificing them on our command is not part of the deal." He had wronged humans once, eliminating the vast majority of their population. He was not going to wrong them again.

"But bandit attacks are causing much loss and suffering to humans as well. Do you not think that they would like to defend themselves?"

"They are free to do so. I allow armed guards, but I will not allow an army. Humans are violent. They will start with the bandits and continue against each other, and soon wars will erupt between the city-states."

Ahn was well aware of his people's bloody history and the terrible things they had done, one that his young mate had no knowledge of. None of the subsequent generations of gods had. It was better that way. As long as they believed that they were peaceful and benevolent people, they would act as such.

It had worked for thousands of years.

But now Mortdh was threatening to destroy that carefully constructed and fiercely maintained illusion.

Far away in his northern stronghold, he did as he pleased, ignoring the laws that had governed the gods, keeping their destructive powers in check since the very beginning of their settlement in this remote corner of the universe.

10

ANNANI

As Annani followed Nai's maid to her mother's private reception room, she wondered what the summons was about. Her lessons with Khiann were supposed to start that same evening, so it probably had to do with that.

Would Nai have some words of wisdom for her? Finally share with her the secrets of seduction?

Doubtful.

It would probably be about what she was not supposed to do while alone with Khiann, and not what she wanted to do. If Annani had her way, there would be very little studying done and a lot of kissing and touching. The question was how many guards her parents would send to keep her from getting what she wanted.

No matter.

Between her powers and Khiann's, they would have no problem thralling a number of guards in a way that would leave no trace and no lingering suspicions.

"You wanted to see me, Mother?" Annani bowed as she entered the chamber.

Gulan, who entered behind her, bowed deeper and then retreated to the back of the room and stood against the wall.

Nai lifted her head and gifted Annani with one of her rare smiles. "Yes, daughter of mine. Please come sit with me."

It was not that her mother was a somber or unhappy goddess, quite the opposite was true. Nai adored Ahn and counted herself the luckiest female for capturing him. But she also loved her role as the ruler's mate, and as such, she had to exude authority, which she interpreted as holding her head high and acting serious at all times, even around her only child.

"I wish to converse with Annani in private." She dismissed Gulan and her own maid.

Gulan looked beyond relieved as she bowed again and left the room.

Nai intimidated her, as she did most people. Knowing how strong her influence on Ahn was, and how much he valued his mate's opinion, gods, as well as immortals and humans, trod lightly around her.

Arranging the folds of her dress, Annani sat on the divan across from her mother, careful to keep her back straight and her chin held high and look as regal as her mother expected her to look at all times. Fates forbid she would dare to slouch, or let an unseemly crease mar the skirt of her dress.

When the maid closed the door behind her and Gulan, Nai cast a soundproofing shroud around the room. "You will do the same every time Khiann is with you," she told Annani.

"Why? It is not as if we are going to be alone."

Nai lifted both brows. "Really? What do you take me for, a fool? Two powerful gods who want to be alone will find a way to do as they please. But you are young and inexperienced, and you might forget that unbeknownst to you someone might be listening in. Always shroud conversations you do not wish overheard."

"Yes, Mother."

Nai reached for a cup of water and took a sip, then put the cup down and sighed. "This talk is long overdue. And since you are about to become intimate with another god, I cannot delay any longer. It is hard for a mother to accept that her little girl is all grown up."

Annani stifled the impulse to roll her eyes. She could not remember her mother ever babying her or treating her as anything other than the future ruler of the realm.

Besides, if Nai was referring to what transpired between a male and a female, they had already had that talk, and Nai had explained the basics of what went where and why.

Her mother had delivered the information in the most dry and technical terms possible. It had not been a very inspiring or motivating talk. If Annani had based her expectation solely on her mother's words, she would have never felt the desire to be intimate with anyone.

Fortunately, her imagination had supplied the missing details, and then a few conversations with her very talkative and not at all bashful seamstress had confirmed what Annani had suspected all along. There was much pleasure to be had, and procreation was not the main goal.

"We already had the talk, Mother."

Nai waved a hand. "Those were only the basic facts. There is so much more."

Duh. "I see. What else can you teach me, Mother?" Annani widened her eyes in mock innocence.

Nai had either not noticed or had chosen to ignore Annani's impudence. "As I explained before, a male god, as well as a male immortal, bites his female during intercourse, mostly around the time he reaches his climax, which is when he fills the female with his male essence."

Great, Nai's delivery was exactly the same it had been the other time. Dry and uninspiring. Ekin had been more passionate when explaining about his improvements to the irrigation system than her mother was when talking about matters of the flesh.

Nai lifted her cup and took another sip of water. "What I have not told you is that the venom of a male god or immortal is addictive."

That was indeed news to Annani. "In what way? Does it make the female crave more intimacy?"

"It does. But if she is intimate with only one male and his venom is the only one to enter her system, she will crave only him and will be repulsed by others."

That did not sound too bad. Annani had no intention of taking on other lovers. She was going to be faithful to Khiann and demand the same from him. And if they were each other's fated trueloves it would not be a problem at all.

She shrugged. "I do not care. I only want Khiann."

Her mother smiled indulgently. "You are infatuated with the boy. That does not necessarily mean love, and certainly not truelove, even though I am sure you are convinced that it does."

Nai was wrong, but Annani had to play along. She had been granted her wish and was going to see Khiann every day. No way was she going to jeopardize this by acting disrespectfully toward her mother.

"That is what the courtship is for. We will explore our feelings for each other."

Nai laughed. "I am sure more than feelings will be explored."

Then her expression turned serious again. "This is exactly what I want to talk to you about. First of all, Khiann's courtship is unofficial. Until the two of you are sure that you are each other's trueloves, Mortdh cannot find out about it. All his spies will report to him is that you have a new tutor."

"A handsome young god. I am sure he is going to get suspicious."

"He might. But Mortdh is not in love with you, and he does not care what you do. What he cares about, though, are appearances. He would not mind too much if you do not remain chaste until you join him, but he would be enraged if you become pregnant and have a child that is not his."

Annani waved a dismissive hand. "The chances of that are so small that it is of no concern. How often do goddesses conceive?"

"Rarely. But it is a possibility. Add to that the certainty of addiction, and you will understand why you should not engage in intercourse with Khiann until you are sure he is the one."

Annani narrowed her eyes. "What exactly does the addiction entail? And how can I avoid it? Most goddesses, other than those who are joined with their truelove, are not monogamous or faithful to their mates. How do they manage that?"

"When a goddess or an immortal female is sexually active, the only way she can avoid addiction to one male is to frequently change partners. A mix of several venoms prevents the addiction to a particular one. Once the addiction sets in, it is impossible for her to be with any male other than the one she is addicted to because she will feel no attraction to anyone else."

"What if something happens to that male? Like what happened to poor Areana's mate? Is that why she is still alone?"

Nai shook her head. "She is alone because she still mourns his death and chooses not to take a new lover. The addiction is long gone. Initially, she must have suffered terrible withdrawal pangs on top of the pain of losing her truelove, but with time they have no doubt subsided. A widow is not sentenced to eternal loneliness."

"What about the males? Do they get addicted as well?" It would be terribly unfair if they did not.

"Eventually, they get addicted too. But it takes less time for the female to succumb than for the male."

Annani crossed her arms over her chest. "This is so unfair."

Nai clasped Annani's hands. "I know, my dear girl. Promise me that you will wait to get intimate with

Khiann until you are certain that he is the one. I do not want you to suffer through withdrawal. I hear that it is terrible."

"I promise."

Since Annani knew with unshakable certainty that Khiann was the one, it had been an easy promise to make. She might wait a week or two to prove it to herself beyond a shadow of a doubt and to comply with her mother's wishes, but not longer than that.

Her attraction to Khiann was too powerful to resist.

PART 3

GARDEN OF LOVE

1

ANNANI

"What do you think of this one?" Annani shook out the skirt of the new blue dress her seamstress had delivered that morning, smoothing out the folds and creases.

The order had been fulfilled with unusual speed. Typically, it took the immortal weeks to be done with the elaborate embroidery adorning Annani's dresses and tunics, not days. For some reason, the seamstress had been exceedingly eager to please this time, and more talkative and full of questions than ever.

Delani was such a gossip.

For a change, however, Annani had been careful, censoring her words and keeping her excitement bottled up, lest the woman suspected something and started asking questions. A lot was at stake and letting a hint slip out could have devastating consequences. Fates forbid Mortdh found out about Khiann's courtship.

Who knew who else the seamstress talked to?

Not everyone was as trustworthy as Gulan, who Annani regarded more as a friend than a servant.

"It is most flattering, my lady." The girl lifted the dresses Annani had tossed over the privacy partition, discarding them as not pretty enough, or too fancy, or not fancy enough.

On the one hand, Annani wanted to look her best for Khiann, but on the other hand, she did not want to appear as if she was trying too hard or showing off her status.

Khiann was going to arrive shortly, for the first time in his official capacity as her tutor. Their non-official, hush-hush courtship period was about to start, and Annani needed to look as tempting and as alluring as possible without it being obvious that she had dedicated much thought to it.

It was such a tough choice.

"Is it nicer than the others?"

"They are all beautiful, my lady, and you look magnificent in every one. I cannot choose one over the other."

Ugh. Gulan probably considered offering her honest opinion as too forward, or maybe she was just indecisive. In either case, her friend was not much help.

Perhaps she should call her guards in. A male's opinion could have been helpful. After all, what looked pleasing to a female's eyes might leave a male indifferent.

Except, asking the guards was inappropriate. Annani treated them as her friends, but unfortunately, they could not reciprocate in kind. There was an invisible and yet very tangible wall of propriety between a princess and her servants. Besides, they would probably react precisely the same as Gulan, saying everything looked beautiful.

Camel droppings. Having an older brother would have been beneficial in so many ways.

Annani chuckled at the absurdity of the thought. If she had an older brother, she would not be in the predicament she was in because she would not be first in line to rule, and Mortdh would not be interested in her. She would be free to mate with whomever she pleased, and her choice would not have the catastrophic potential of starting a war.

Indeed, an older brother could have been the answer to much more significant problems than choosing a dress to wear for Khiann.

Maybe in the absence of a brother an uncle would do?

Annani could ask Ekin. Her father's older and much more fun half-brother was probably the only person she trusted to tell her the truth. Even her parents told her only what they thought she should know. Which she thought was dishonest and cast a shadow on her relationship with them. In Annani's opinion, omitting information, especially when it pertained to her, was almost as bad as lying.

Ekin always answered her questions to the best of his ability.

Besides, he knew about her and Khiann, which meant that stifling her excitement would not be necessary around him. Annani wanted to dance and sing and tell everyone how happy she was.

Instead, she had to act as though nothing unusual was going on.

Except, her uncle's quarters were situated on the other side of the palace, and asking him to come to her chamber would border on disrespectful. On the other hand, crossing the palace with each new dress she wanted his opinion on was too time-consuming, and she was in a bit of a rush.

It seemed Gulan would have to do.

With a sigh, Annani tried a different approach. "Which color do you think looks best on me?"

"All colors look good on you, my lady. But personally, I think red hues complement your complexion the best."

Annani peeked from behind the partition. "Are you sure? Even with my red hair?"

Gulan shrugged. "I am not an expert. Perhaps I should get the seamstress?"

That could have been an excellent idea if Annani had the time. After all, Delani was her primary source of information on everything that had to do with the male sex. If nothing else, a few giggles over some racy stories might have calmed the flurry of butterflies taking flight in Annani's stomach.

"Hand me the burgundy one," she told her maid. The dress was not new, but she had worn it only once before. The fabric was beautiful, soft and airy, which was vitally important since Annani did not do well in the heat, especially when she was excited, and the air was still hot out in the gardens.

Sweating was most unbecoming, and it would be

several more hours before the night cooled sufficiently to be comfortable.

Since the fabric of the dress was unadorned, Annani added a gold necklace, a matching pair of earrings, and a circlet to hold her hair back.

"Not bad," she told the reflection in the mirror. She was not overdressed or underdressed, and she looked pretty.

"Perfect," Gulan sighed. "Master Khiann is going to swoon."

Annani huffed. "Male gods do not swoon." On second thought, though, she giggled thinking that he might get a little dizzy if all the blood from his big body rushed into a certain part of him.

Knowing Gulan, though, that had not been what had prompted her comment. The girl was too innocent to entertain thoughts of that nature.

"My apologies, my lady." Gulan bowed.

"No apologies required." Annani pulled her friend into a quick embrace. "You are my best friend. I want you to always speak your mind when we are alone."

As Gulan returned the hug, her long, strong arms were as gentle as those of a mother embracing a child. "And you are mine. But I cannot behave one way when we are alone and another when we are not. It is too confusing. I love you in my heart, but whether anyone else is present or not, I prefer to always address you with the respect and deference you deserve. It makes matters simpler for me."

"Oh, Gulan." Annani stretched on the tips of her toes and kissed her friend's cheek. "I am so lucky to have you. I would have been so lonely without you." Hiring

Gulan as her handmaid and protector was the best thing Annani's parents had done for her. Other than giving her life, of course.

A lone tear slid down Gulan's cheek. "Thank you." Embarrassed, she quickly wiped the tear and forced a smile. "My apologies for getting overly emotional."

Annani patted her shoulder. "Your big heart is one of the things I love most about you. Feel free to get emotional whenever you feel like it."

Gulan was a big softy who got teary-eyed over cute babies and fluffy kittens and true love stories.

A moment later there was a quiet knock on the door, followed by a hesitant, "My lady?"

"What is it? You can come in, Gumer."

The guard opened the door just enough to stick his head through it. "Your tutor has arrived, my lady. He is waiting for you in the gazebo as you have instructed."

"Thank you. I will be out in a minute," Annani said.

Gumer bowed and closed the door.

Taking a deep breath, she smoothed the skirt of her dress once again.

"Okay, one last look in the mirror." Satisfied with her appearance, Annani turned to Gulan. "Shall we?"

2

KHIANN

"Stop stressing, you look fine." Esag tugged on Khiann's tunic. It was a little tight at the chest, which caused it to ride up. He had bulked up since it had been made for him several moon cycles before.

"Fine is not good enough."

"How about dashingly handsome?"

Khiann smiled. "Better. But the tunic is too tight. Maybe I should wear a different one?"

It was the best casual garment he owned. The others were either too fancy or too plain. Up until today, Khiann had not concerned himself with clothing, and whatever his mother ordered for him had been fine. Except, he was about to court a princess and needed to look the part.

"It shows off your muscles. Girls like a muscular chest."

"Is that so?" Khiann gave the tunic another tug and puffed up the aforementioned body part, putting even more strain on the seams. The stitching held.

Good. It would have been embarrassing to have the garment tear in Annani's presence.

"You look irresistible, my lord," Esag taunted in a feminine tone while fanning himself with his hand.

"Now look at what you have done." Khiann batted his eyelashes. "You made me blush."

As Esag had no doubt intended, the teasing had lightened the mood, easing the churning in Khiann's gut. Judging by his nervousness, one might think he was a blushing virgin and not an experienced young god who had bedded females aplenty and had not heard a single complaint yet.

If anyone should be nervous, it was Annani.

He wondered what she was doing. Was she standing in front of her mirror the same as he was and fretting about her appearance?

Not that she had anything to worry about. He would think her the most beautiful female ever born no matter how she was dressed. Even a commoner's garb looked good on her.

Taking one last glance at the mirror, Khiann gave his tunic another tug for good measure and raked his fingers through his shoulder-length hair, pushing the wavy strands behind his ears. It still looked messy.

"Hand me the comb, Esag."

His squire shook his head. "You do not want to appear too well-groomed. Girls go for the carefree, tousled style." Esag demonstrated by pushing his fingers through his own dark hair and then tossing his head from side to side. "I present the wind-blown style."

"More like the just-fell-out-of-bed style." Nevertheless, Khiann decided to take Esag's advice and forgo the comb. "Let us go. I do not want to be late."

They walked to the palace instead of riding their horses, first of all because Khiann did not want the animal smell clinging to his clothes, and secondly because he figured his visit would draw less attention if they arrived on foot.

As they entered the palace's inner courtyard, Gulan waved at them from the front door, then blushed furiously when Esag bowed to her in greeting.

"Good evening, Master Khiann." She bowed. "My lady awaits you in the gazebo."

"Thank you, and good evening to you as well. Please, lead the way." Khiann waved his hand.

"How are you, Gulan?" Esag asked.

"I am well," the girl answered without looking at the squire, bowed again, and then quickly turned on her heel.

As she walked briskly toward the gardens, Khiann and Esag followed a couple of steps behind her.

The nervous energy radiating from Gulan was palpable, and Khiann was quite sure that it had nothing to do with Annani and his first official tutoring session, and everything to do with his squire.

He needed to have a talk with Esag about leading the girl on. If the guy cared about Gulan even a little, he should dial down the charm and act indifferent. At first, her feelings might get hurt, but it would be better for her in the long run. The girl should set her sights on an available immortal, not one who was promised to another.

As they reached the gazebo, and Khiann got his first

glimpse of Annani, all thoughts of Gulan and Esag were forgotten. She looked resplendent in her dark red dress, the soft fabric hugging her lush body most enticingly. Annani was small and not at all voluptuous, but every part of her was made to perfection.

Fates, how he wanted to pull her into his arms and run his hands all over those slender feminine curves. But courtship was not about the meeting of bodies, or at least it was not supposed to be. It was supposed to be about the meetings of minds and hearts and about ascertaining compatibility.

In theory.

In reality, males were slaves to their baser natures and filled with carnal thoughts. He would do his best, though, and hope it was enough.

Khiann bowed. "Greetings, my lady."

With a tiny smirk, Annani inclined her head in a perfunctory bow. "Good evening, Master Khiann. I am eager for our first lesson to begin."

"Yes, indeed." Khiann pulled out his tablet from his satchel and put it on the stone table. "I prepared a list of the goods currently imported and also of those exported."

Annani clapped her hands. "Splendid. It sounds fascinating." Taking a seat on the bench, she motioned for him to join her.

"Come on, Gulan." Esag took the maid's elbow. "While these two discuss commerce, I am going to teach you how to defend yourself and your lady."

The girl glanced at Annani. "Do I have your permission to leave, my lady?"

"Yes. You should have taken combat lessons a long

time ago. Size and physical strength are not enough to stave off an attack."

Gulan's dark complexion got a shade darker and ruddier. "As you command, my lady." She executed a slight bow before letting Esag lead her down the meandering garden path.

As the two walked away, Khiann leaned and whispered in Annani's ear, "You should not encourage this. Esag is promised to another."

Annani's face fell. "That is such a shame. Gulan is quite taken with him."

"I have noticed. I will have a talk with him."

"Poor Gulan. She is going to be crushed, especially since Esag seems to genuinely like her." Annani sighed. "People should be free to choose their mates. I do not support the custom of parents arranging their children's engagements at a young age. It is a loophole that allows them to circumvent the law of consent. I do not know how loving parents can sentence their child to a loveless joining."

Khiann took her hand. "Of course you do not. You are a victim of that custom."

A slight, barely there rustle of leaves reminded Khiann that he should have cast a shroud around them before speaking so freely. It could have been nothing more than a bird in a tree, but it could have also been one of Mortdh's spies.

Concentrating, he cast a complicated shroud, creating not only a sound barrier but also an illusion of Annani and him poring over his tablet. As soon as it was in place, he turned to his princess and smiled. "Are you ready for your first lesson, my love?"

Annani gasped. "Did you just call me your love?"

"Yes, I did." He took her hand and brought it to his lips for a kiss. "I have fallen for you, my feisty sprite."

"But our courtship has not even begun yet."

"I know what is in my heart. I have known it for a very long time and tried to ignore it because I thought there was not the slightest chance of anything ever coming of it. But now that you have given me that chance, I am going to prove to you that I am your one and only."

With a soft sigh, Annani lifted their joined hands and kissed the back of his. "You do not have to prove anything to me. I already know that we are fated to be joined for eternity."

3

GULAN

Gods help me, Gulan thought as she reluctantly let Esag lead her away.

Annani had been too preoccupied with Khiann to notice the desperate plea in Gulan's eyes, which had been begging for the opposite of what her words had been asking for. She had not wanted to leave with the squire. She could not handle being alone with him.

Was this love? Or was this illness?

Immortals did not get sick, so it must have been the former.

Did Annani suffer from sweaty palms, racing heartbeat, difficulty breathing, and nausea?

Gulan did not think so. Annani might have exhibited a few signs of nervous excitement, but at no point had her lady been close to fainting as Gulan was now.

The effect of Esag's proximity was not enjoyable. If that was how love or attraction or whatever that was felt, then it was poisonous.

"This looks like a good spot." Esag pointed to a clearing in the garden. "We can practice here."

Her throat too tight for talking, Gulan nodded.

"I am going to show you a few basic moves." He retook her elbow and positioned her in the center of the dirt patch delineated by bushes. "Stand here."

He took a step back and looked at her hands, which were clasped tightly together. "You need to loosen up. Drop your arms by your sides and shake them like you are shaking water off." He demonstrated.

She imitated him. "Like this?" Her voice came out barely louder than a whisper.

"Yes. That is good. Now do the same with your legs." He winked. "One leg at a time. I do not want you to fall on your pretty face."

At the compliment, Gulan felt her face heat up even worse. She was probably redder than a pomegranate.

Once she was done shaking out her legs, he had her shake her arms again. Gulan felt silly but did as he instructed. Not one to argue or assert herself, she did all that he asked of her. Besides, if she cooperated, the training session would be over sooner rather than later. She could go to the fountain and splash some water on her burning cheeks before returning to Annani.

"Now you are ready." Esag smiled. "I am going to show you the first basic move. Pretend you want to grab me."

"Grab you where?"

He patted his chest. "Pretend you are a thug and grab my tunic here."

Hesitantly, she reached for his tunic, but before she could grab a fistful, Esag caught her wrist and pulled her forward while turning around in slow motion. "I do not want to complete the move, but the idea is to use your opponent's momentum and throw him over your shoulder."

That did not make any sense. "Why would I want to carry him on my shoulder?"

Esag laughed. "I meant to throw him over, so he hits the ground, not keep him there."

"Oh."

"I would have demonstrated, but I do not want to hurt you."

That defied the purpose of the lesson. If she was already there and suffering Esag's disturbing proximity, she should at least learn a few moves.

"I am not easily hurt. Please show me how it is done because I do not understand what you mean."

"Are you sure? I am going to throw you on the ground, and it is going to hurt your back, and your tunic is going to get dirty."

It felt good to be treated like a girl. Not many people did, most expecting her to act like a boy just because she was as tall and as strong as one. Gulan did not like it, but she was used to it, and to gain the ability to protect her lady better, she was willing to suffer much worse than an aching back and dirty clothes.

Those were nothing.

The problem was Esag. Touching him, and getting touched by him. She was not herself around him. A different teacher would have been preferable. Except, she could not back out now without offending him.

Besides, no one else had offered to train her, and she was too shy to ask one of the guards, or any male for that matter. It would have been nice to have a female warrior to teach her, but there were none.

Females did not train for combat.

"Do not worry about me. It is my duty and obligation to protect my lady to the best of my ability. I want to learn."

"As you wish." Esag did not look or sound sure. "I will try to make your fall as gentle as possible."

"Do not." She wanted to add that she was a big girl and could take it, but that was kind of obvious and nothing she wished to emphasize.

For the first time in Gulan's life, a male was showing interest in her, and not just any male, a handsome squire who could have any girl he wanted. If he found her desirable, she was not going to point out why she was not.

"Try to grab my tunic again." He pointed at his chest.

Taking a deep breath, Gulan lurched forward, hoping to catch Esag before he had time to react, but his reflexes were fast, and he grabbed her wrist the same way he had done before, only this time he did not stop.

Turning, he gave a mighty pull on her arm and swept her leg from under her with his. For one short moment, she was draped over his back, and in the next, she was flying heels over head in the air. With a loud thud, she landed on the ground.

Still holding on to her wrist, Esag straddled her, a knee on each side. "This is how you make sure your opponent does not get up. You sit on him."

"You are not sitting on me." Thank the gods for that.

"No, I am not." He jumped up, helping her to her feet

by pulling on her wrist again. "But you get what I mean."

Gulan nodded, then patted her tunic to dislodge the leaves and dirt clinging to its back.

"Are you all right?" Esag asked.

"Yes. I think I can do it."

He turned her around and patted her back to clean the rest of the dirt off her, making her blush again as his hand brushed against her bottom.

Did he do it on purpose?

Gods, she hoped not.

When he was done, Esag walked over to the middle of the clearing. "I am heavy, and you may not be able to lift me. Use my momentum and put your back into it."

Was he teasing her? Esag had seen her lift a boy and throw him across the schoolyard without using any technique. This was going to be easy.

On second thought, though, maybe she should pretend and fail on purpose?

It was not feminine to be so strong.

The thing was, Gulan hated to lie and was exceedingly bad at it, which was the main reason why Annani's shenanigans were so difficult for her. Duplicity of any kind was foreign to her nature. Even keeping secrets was an effort.

She would have to throw him. The other thing that bothered her was where exactly was Esag going to grab her? She could not point at her chest as he had.

"I am sure that I can throw you over my shoulder."

"We will see. Drape your braid over your front. I am going to pretend as if I am going for it."

Thank the gods Esag solved that dilemma.

She followed his instructions, pulling her heavy braid and draping it over her left breast. Hopefully, she could catch Esag's wrist before his hand reached her. What if he got ahold of more than her hair?

As his eyes followed her movements, they lingered on her chest for a moment too long before returning to her face. Apparently, the same thought had crossed his mind.

"Are you ready?" he asked.

Gulan nodded.

Esag did not move as fast as she had expected him to, giving her ample time to catch his wrist before his hand could close around her braid.

Another thing she had not expected was for her pull to be so strong that she did not need to trip his leg in order to send him flying over her shoulder. If not for her hand still holding onto his wrist, Esag would have landed in the bushes bordering the clearing.

As it was, he landed on the ground with a mighty thud and a loud grunt.

Gulan stopped his forward movement, letting go of his wrist only when she was sure he would not slide further away. As she straddled him, her knees on either side of him, her long tunic rode up her thighs.

Esag smiled up at her as if he was the one who had emerged triumphant, his hands landing on her thighs. "Gods, you are beautiful. I could stare into those green eyes of yours for eternity."

That was the last thing Gulan had expected him to say. She had been ready for comments about her strength, or about her heavy weight on top of him. She had even braced for a disgusted expression or a sour one. But not this.

For a moment, she remained frozen, looking into Esag's smiling eyes, terrified by how good his hands felt on her thighs.

What was she supposed to say? That she found him beautiful as well? That she could stare into those smiling eyes of his for eternity too?

Instead, she bolted upright and ran.

"Gulan!" Esag called after her. "Wait! What happened?" He chased her, the sound of his flopping sandals thundering in her ears.

She wished she could put the storm of feelings raging inside her into words or at least calm down for long enough to answer him, but it was no use.

Gulan just kept on running.

4

KHIANN

As Annani let go of Khiann's hand, he clasped it again. "I need to keep touching you."

"Someone might see us."

"I added a visual shroud to the sound barrier. Anyone passing by will see us sitting with our heads bent over my tablet and will think we are studying. We can do whatever we want as long as we are inside the gazebo."

Annani's demeanor changed in an instant, the seductive smirk and smiling eyes hinting at her intentions. "Anything we want?"

My princess is not shy. Thank you, wise Fates.

Other males might have preferred a demure mate, but Khiann did not. Annani's assertiveness and commanding presence excited him, challenged him, and made him eager to play. With her, there would not be a dull moment.

In one swift move, he lifted her off the bench and onto his lap. "Anything your heart desires."

She cupped his cheek. "My heart and my body are in accord in their desires. I want your lips on mine and your hands all over me."

Dear Fates, the girl was temptation personified. Khiann had a feeling she would not object if he threw her over the table and had his way with her.

Was he the luckiest of gods or what?

But even though the hard rod in his breeches disagreed, it was too soon for that. Annani was an untried virgin, and despite her bravado had a lot to learn about intimacy and what it entailed.

According to the sensual arts teacher his father had hired for him, a female required a buildup of intimacy and trust before surrendering her body to a male, and the first time was the most important one. If the experience were fulfilling, both emotionally and physically, it would set a positive tone for the future. Conversely, a less than satisfactory first experience had the potential of ruining her expectations and making her less than enthusiastic for repeats.

His teacher had warned Khiann to take his time with females, especially the young and inexperienced ones. Even when the girl was impatient and implied that she was ready, it was not always so. It was his responsibility to ascertain that she was.

People were not animals, she had said, and the sexual act was not only about fulfilling basic needs and procreation. Without the heart and the mind, the joining was not as satisfying.

Her teachings had served Khiann well. He had not been in love with any of his former partners, but he had never taken to bed a female he had not liked or one that he had not felt some sort of a connection with.

How much more fulfilling would the experience be with the one he loved? No doubt unimaginably so.

Provided he exercised restraint.

It would be a mistake to succumb too soon because his sprite was in a hurry to sample the fruits of passion. Too much was at stake. They had eternity to enjoy each other, and he was going to make sure that they started it right, which meant following his teacher's advice to the letter.

By the time he joined with Annani, he would know her soul, and her heart and her body's every response to every touch better than he knew his own.

Lifting his hand, he gently rubbed his finger over her lush lower lip, then bent his head and kissed her, just a soft, featherlight kiss.

"You smell like sunshine and first rain," he murmured against her lips.

She giggled. "What is the difference between the first and the second rain? And I did not know sunshine had a smell."

"It is how I imagine the scents of happiness and vitality."

"Oh. It sounds nice." She leaned into him, pressing her small body against his chest as if seeking to touch as much of him as possible. "You smell like thunder and lightning."

"I did not know they had a smell."

As Khiann held her to him, his palm slowly sliding up and down her exposed back, he applauded her choice of dress. It allowed him to touch her bare skin which was as soft as a petal and as smooth as silk.

"That is how I imagine the scents of power and vigor." Annani closed her eyes and submitted to his soft touches, her back muscles relaxing under his hands. "It feels so good," she mumbled into his chest. "I feel so close to you. Closer than I ever felt to anyone."

His heart swelling with love, he kissed her forehead. "I feel the same way."

"But as good as this is, I ache for more." She sighed and put her hand over her flat belly. "There is hunger in me that only you can satisfy."

Clever sprite, she was redirecting their conversation to where she wanted it to go.

"Have you ever satisfied yourself?" he asked.

Annani chuckled. "Many times, and more so since I saw you again in the throne room. I do not want it to go to your head, but you have been the star of all my girly fantasies."

He leaned back. "All of them? You have never thought of another male?"

"No, only you." She leaned away and looked up at him. "I have been loyal to you even in my dreams, and it makes me angry to think that you were not." She pouted and looked away.

Fates, if he had known that he would never have touched another female. But then he would have been just as inexperienced as she was and could not teach her all the marvels of the sensual arts he had learned.

"I am so sorry, but I have not dared to even dream of you because you were an impossible dream. If I had known, I would have waited." Khiann hooked a finger under her chin and forced her to look at him. "I do not know if this is any consolation to you, but I think of my former partners as teachers who prepared me for you so I could bring you the most pleasure. Can you think of them in the same way?"

"Teachers, huh?" She smiled. "I prefer it to lovers, that is for sure. I am still jealous, but I understand why it is unreasonable for me to wish you had not partaken. Besides, I like it that you are well-versed in the sensual arts. I feel safe in your hands."

A laugh shook her small frame. "Now it is your turn to tutor me, and I have to wonder if that was what my father had in mind when he commissioned you."

"Your father is not naive. I am sure he knows what he is allowing and that my tutelage is not limited to commerce."

"Perhaps he expects you to behave yourself?"

It was Khiann's turn to laugh. "Even if he expects that of me, he does not expect it from you, his head-strong and impetuous princess."

As Annani opened her mouth to answer, Khiann's head snapped in the direction of a suspicious sound. He was quite sure it had not been made by a small creature or a bird. "Shh." He put his finger to her lips. "Listen."

They should have been safe in the gazebo. Other than another god, no one should be able to penetrate his shroud.

In theory.

Some immortals were almost as powerful as the average god, and conversely, some gods were less powerful than the most talented of immortals. It was a secret the gods kept to themselves, lest the immortals get ideas they should not.

A moment later he caught a flash of a woman's skirt peeking from behind a tree, and then immediately darting back.

Annani waved a dismissive hand. "It is only my seamstress. She probably delivered my new dresses, but does not want to disturb us while we are studying."

"Is she a human or an immortal?"

"An immortal."

"Are you sure she is not here to spy on us?"

Annani shrugged. "I cannot be sure of anyone. Although, in Delani's case, she might be spying for herself and not for Mortdh. The woman is an incorrigible gossip."

"Do you want me to drop the shroud so you can see what she wants?"

With a sigh, Annani lifted off Khiann's lap and sat next to him. "First, let us assume the same pose as in the illusion. I would rather deal with her and have her gone before we resume our lesson." She winked. "I want my entire focus to be on my teacher."

He could not argue with that logic.

"As you wish, my beautiful flower."

5

ANNANI

As Khiann let his shroud dissipate, Annani lifted her head and called out. "Delani? Is that you?"

The seamstress stepped out from behind the tree. "I am so sorry to disturb you, my lady, but I could not remember whether you wanted the flower embroidery on the yellow dress or the blue one."

That was odd. Annani remembered the seamstress taking notes as she usually did, using charcoal on a clay tablet. Only gods possessed tablets, everyone else had to use more primitive writing implements.

She narrowed her eyes at the woman. "What happened to the notes you took?"

"I am so sorry, my lady. My son thought it was an old clay tablet and used it to do his homework. He erased my notes, and I could not remember if the flowers went on the yellow dress or the blue."

A reasonable enough explanation, and the scent of guilt might have been because of the mishap and not because of some nefarious spying activity.

Still, Annani decided to further censor her conversations with the seamstress, maybe even supply the woman with misleading information.

"The flowers go on the yellow dress and the waves pattern on the blue."

"Thank you, my lady." Delani bowed. "My sincere apologies for disturbing your lesson."

Annani waved a hand. "Apology accepted. Now, off with you, Master Khiann has better things to do than hear about my new dresses."

"Yes, my lady." The seamstress retreated while bowing. "My apologies to you and to Lord Khiann." She turned and ran the rest of the way.

Khiann waited a few moments before recasting the shroud. "Do you believe her?" he asked after the gazebo had been secured.

"I do not know. Her explanation sounded reasonable, and the scent of guilt was appropriate to her offense. I think it would have been much stronger if she was spying for Mortdh."

"Maybe yes and maybe no. I have heard of immortals who could regulate their scents, and I have encountered a human once who emitted none at all."

"Is that possible? Everyone emits emotional scents, even gods."

Khiann shrugged. "Anomalies exist. Just as someone can be born without the sense of smell, or blind, or deaf, another can lack the ability to produce smells. Your seamstress could be one of those who can control how much smell they emit, or she might be one of those people who believe in the stories they tell. In either case, I suggest caution around her."

"I agree. I plan on going a step further and feeding her misleading information."

He arched a brow. "Like what?"

"I can say that you are a horribly boring teacher and that I cannot wait for the lessons to be over. I can even make a few remarks about another god or gods who I find attractive."

He narrowed his eyes at her. "Like who?"

Oh, this was going to be fun. Let Khiann feel some jealousy for a change. She should not be the only one afflicted by that most disturbing and uncomfortable malady.

"Like Cahn. He is so tall, and you know I have a weakness for tall males. Then there is Bodhn, not a god, only an immortal, but what a physique. All those muscles and those piercing blue eyes." She sighed dramatically, enjoying the red hue creeping up Khiann's cheeks. "He is so mouth-watering that even goddesses pursue him."

Watching the red spreading to Khiann's ears whetted Annani's appetite for more teasing. "And there is Toven, Ekin's younger son. He is not as gorgeous as some of the other gods, but he has a beautiful mind. He is smart and kind and loyal, the complete opposite of his older half-brother. If my father had promised me to him, I would not have minded as much, even though he is not my truelove mate."

Apparently, the last comment was one too far. Khiann was fuming. "Really? Maybe you could go to your father and renegotiate?"

Annani put on a mock sad expression. "Toven is happily joined, and he is loyal to his mate."

"What if he were not?"

She playfully flicked Khiann's nose with her finger. "Then you would have a serious competitor for my affections."

"Is that so?" Khiann lifted her up, but instead of pulling her into his lap, he draped her over it and smacked her behind.

Annani turned her head and smirked at his angry face. "Jealous?" she taunted.

"Yes, I am." He flipped the back of her dress up, exposing her naked bottom, and smacked it again, then repeated it on the other cheek.

It did not hurt at all. If anything, it was arousing. Khiann could see not only her bare cheeks, but also her femininity blooming between them.

His sharp inhale confirmed that he had seen the effect, or smelled it. Annani had been told that the scent of a goddess's desire was most pleasing to her male counterpart and acted as a powerful aphrodisiac.

As Khiann's palm rested on the fleshy part of her upturned behind, Annani waited with breathless anticipation for his next move.

Would he caress her heated flesh?

What she wanted most was for his fingers to find her moist center and touch her the way she had touched herself when thinking of him. It would no doubt feel a thousand times better when he did it.

"Beautiful," he said, smoothing his palm down the curve of her buttocks.

She almost cried out when Khiann stopped a fraction of a finger away from where she wanted him to touch her.

What was he waiting for?

With the haze of her desire clouding her thoughts, it took a moment until it occurred to her that he might be waiting for her permission.

"Touch me," she breathed.

A single finger feathered over her nether lips, as if he was afraid his touch might break her.

"More." Well aware that her request sounded more like a command, Annani was too needy to care. The hunger building up inside her was frightening in its intensity. If she did not get immediate relief, she was going to explode.

Leaning over her, Khiann kissed one buttock and then the other before blowing softly on the hot flesh in between them. "I want to lick that sweet nectar you have made for me. Is that all right?"

Had there ever been a more rhetorical question than that?

It was more than all right. It was necessary.

"Yes," she whispered. When he did not respond immediately, she added, "Please."

Holding both cheeks in his large hands, Khiann delved his tongue inside her. His gentle lick had the effect of a bolt of lighting on her.

Annani jerked up and away.

The sensation was too much, too intense, and she had not been prepared for her body's response. It was like nothing she had experienced before using her own fingers.

"Too much, too soon?" Khiann asked.

"I did not expect it to feel like that."

"Good or bad?"

"Good. Definitely good."

"Okay then."

When he licked her again, she forced herself to stay still.

With a soft sigh, Khiann kissed her bottom and then lifted her up and hugged her to his chest.

Bewildered, she asked, "Why did you stop?"

"You are not ready, my love. Your beautiful bottom scrambled my brains, and I jumped ahead, skipping over several necessary steps."

What was he talking about?

"What steps? I liked your tongue on me."

"At the least, I should have kissed you first."

She had not been aware that a particular sequence had to be followed. Her seamstress had not mentioned it when describing the many pleasures of the flesh, and neither had her mother.

But given the fact that Khiann had been schooled in the sensual arts by experts, he probably knew better how things needed to progress to maximize her pleasure. Annani trusted him more than her female sources of information.

"Then kiss me now and then quickly follow with the other steps."

He chuckled. "Annani, my love, you have no idea how precious you are."

6

KHIANN

It took a lot of effort for Khiann to stifle the laugh bubbling up from his chest—or more precisely from his overflowing heart. The unexpected mirth had also helped the situation with his fangs, which had now retracted to their normal size.

For a few moments, he had been very close to the danger zone, the predator in him threatening to overwhelm the thinking man. The sight of Annani's naked flesh and the evidence of her desire for him had tested his restraint.

Holding her to him, he had been struggling with the need to sink his fangs into her. Thankfully, the remainder of her inexperience and innocence had cooled him down.

Annani was like a child, who in her eagerness for the candy had resigned herself to eating her vegetables first and getting that necessary evil out of the way as quickly as possible. What she did not know, however, was that without eating her veggies first, the candy would not taste as good.

Reluctantly, he lifted her up a little and tugged down her dress, restoring her modesty. "Patience, my beautiful flower. There is a lot of pleasure in prolonging the buildup and exercising self-denial."

Leaning away, she eyed him as if he were out of his mind. "I do not see how it makes any sense. I know what I want, and I want it now."

Khiann shook his head. "Do you trust me?"

From the rebellious gleam in her eyes, Annani knew where he was leading and did not like it. She crossed her arms over her chest and tilted her chin up, affecting an imperious expression. "I have no choice but to trust you." Releasing one arm, she waved it in front of his face. "You are the one who has been taught by experts and has all the experience. I am only a naive virgin." Annani huffed and returned her arm to where it had been before.

Feisty sprite.

Khiann loved Annani's spunk and her spirit, but the flip side was that she was not as pliable and accommodating as the other women he had been with. He was used to females who were eager to please him and thought little of their own pleasure. It had been up to him to ensure they had received as much or more than they had given.

But then he had never been with a goddess.

Of course, she would be more demanding than those who considered themselves inferior to gods.

Except, Khiann had a feeling Annani's assertiveness

had nothing to do with her godly heritage. It was not even the result of her upbringing as the next ruler. It was her nature. She was born with it.

"I will make you a deal," he said.

Annani narrowed her eyes. "What kind of a deal?"

"Until our third joining, you will have to obey my instructions and follow my rules of sensual engagement without question. It will give you time to learn what is pleasing to you and what is not. I do not want you to rush things. As I have said before, the anticipation enhances the pleasure."

She lifted a brow. "And after our third joining, you will obey my instructions and follow my rules without question?"

He would not like it, but it was only fair. "Yes."

Considering his proposal, Annani tapped a finger on her lips. "What if I do not know what I want even after the third joining?"

"Then you will command me to continue teaching you."

With a soft sigh, Annani uncrossed her arms and put her cheek on his chest. "I am confused, I will admit it."

He caressed her back. "About what, my love?"

"On the one hand, it excites me when you take charge, and I yield to you, but on the other hand, I want you to do exactly what I have in mind, at the exact moment I want it. I know it does not make any sense, and not only because of the contradiction. You are not a mind reader. Also, I do not wish to be selfish. I want to know what pleases you as well."

Perfection. He loved that she was not afraid to reveal

her innermost thoughts. In fact, it seemed that Annani was not afraid of anything.

His courageous princess.

Before answering, he palmed her nape and kissed her long and hard, leaving her panting and breathless when he was done.

"I do not need to be a mind reader to fulfill your desires. It is my pleasure as well as my duty to learn your every little response and know your body and mind better than you know it yourself. Because you are inexperienced, you need to learn it as well. The art of sensual pleasure is not a theoretical study. It can only be learned by experiencing and experimenting, preferably with one who has reached mastery in the field."

Annani chuckled. "I will make you a deal."

That should be interesting. "Yes?"

"I will agree to your deal provided you never mention your prior experiences again. I would rather pretend that you were born with the knowledge."

He was not going to get a better one than that. "Agreed."

Annani wrapped her arms around his neck and lifted her head. "Let us seal the deal with another kiss."

Evidently, agreeing to the deal and actually following his rules were not one and the same. Annani could not go against her nature. But she would learn.

"I will let it slide this time, but from now on I am the one giving out instructions. Is that clear?" He arched a brow.

"Sorry. Old habits and all that. I will try to hold my tongue and practice obedience until our third joining.

Hopefully, it will not take too long to reach that pinnacle." She winked at him.

"Imp." He tweaked her nose. The earth's core would freeze over before Annani learned obedience, but it would be fun watching her try.

7

ESAG

"Can you come with me?" Esag asked Khiann.

"To court Ashegan? Have you lost your mind?"

"Please? I cannot stand being alone with her." The girl talked and talked and talked. If he were a human, he would have gotten a headache.

Khiann shook his head. "You need to break off the engagement. Imagine an eternity of misery being mated to someone you cannot stand."

Esag scratched the back of his head. "I wish I could, but my family needs this. My father has gained a lot of business connections thanks to Ashegan's father, and my sisters have better chances of securing good mates. If I break the engagement, all of it would be lost. It would ruin my family."

"I understand. You have explained all of that before, but you did not tell me you were actually suffering in her company. It is one thing to be joined with someone you do not love, and another thing altogether to be joined to someone you cannot stand. In the first case, love can come later, which is not likely in the second."

"That is what concubines and mistresses are for." Esag winked. "You will have to raise my pay." As Khiann's squire, he was earning decent wages but not enough to support a wife and a mistress.

The thing was, everyone expected Esag to leave Khiann's employ after the joining and start working for Ashegan's father. The pay would be much better, and after learning the ins and outs of the metalworking business, he could open a shop of his own. Not a bad life for an immortal from a lowly family. All he had to sacrifice for it was joining with an annoying woman.

Besides, Ashegan might mature into someone he could at least tolerate. After all, she was pleasant to look at, and if he stuffed his ears with wool, he would not have to listen to her either. She would not even notice because their conversations were one-sided. She talked, and he pretended to listen, smiling and nodding from time to time.

It was safer that way.

The girl got offended by everything and cried over nothing. Esag had given up on having a normal conversation with her a long time ago.

"I should be going. If I am late even a little, Ashegan will take offense and cry."

Khiann put down his tablet and looked up at him. "What if you could secure another joining that is beneficial to your family? Find a nice immortal girl who will not drive you crazy?"

"Too late for that. Besides, Ashegan is the best I can get. Her father must have known she would grow up to be an intolerable female and made sure her intended could not run off."

Khiann tried to hide the pity in his eyes by looking down at his tablet. "Good luck, my friend. Maybe she will change for the better after the joining."

"I hope." Esag bowed. "I will see you tomorrow morning."

"Esag!" Khiann called after him.

"Yes?"

"Remember what I have told you about keeping 'you know what' a secret."

Esag put his hand over his heart. "I have sworn it on my immortal life, my lord. Your secret is safe with me."

"Very well."

It was a testament to their friendship that Khiann had confided in him about his secret courtship of Annani.

The lucky bastard.

Luck seemed to follow the rich and the powerful. Khiann was courting the woman he loved, one who also happened to be the future ruler of their people.

Would Ahn have agreed to the courtship if Khiann was the son of a poor family instead of the richest? Not that any of the other gods were poor. As heads of city-states, they collected taxes and were rich without doing much.

Except, Esag did not envy Khiann his future bride, he envied Khiann's ability to choose. Annani was stunning, probably the most beautiful goddess of them all, but she was a handful.

Esag liked demure girls. Not subservient, but feminine, quiet, and well-mannered.

Like Gulan.

The girl had run off on him when he had told her she was beautiful. Chasing after her all the way back to the gazebo, he had been surprised at her speed. Apparently, Gulan was not only as strong as a male but could run just as fast.

When he had finally caught up with her, he could not ask her what troubled her in front of the two gods. She had refused to even look at him.

For some reason, his compliment had scared her away or offended her. Had she thought he had lied?

It was true that most males would not have thought of Gulan as feminine, but that was because they looked at her tall frame and did not bother to look at her beautiful face and gorgeous eyes.

Esag could see nothing else.

Well, that was not entirely true. The girl was blessed with an impressive pair of breasts that he could not wait to put his hands on. And he had noticed her legs as well. They were long and strong.

Last night he had pleasured himself while fantasizing about those legs wrapped around his middle, squeezing as he thrust into her.

Damnation. Esag's steps faltered as he hardened and had to adjust himself.

Gulan was precisely the type of girl he would have chosen for himself if he were free to do so. Her size and strength aside, she had a very mellow character, was polite to a fault, and as demure as they came. She was not stupid or vacuous either.

Perhaps he could convince her to become his concubine. He could build a separate life with her, treating her as well as he would an official mate. And if Ashegan retaliated by taking lovers of her own, he would not mind at all.

It could work.

Gods and immortals were not known for their fidelity, and arrangements like that were common. Except for the truelove couples, most everyone took lovers on the side; some did it only occasionally, while others opted for more permanent arrangements.

Gulan was not a daughter of a prominent family, and given her unusual physical attributes, her chances of a good mating were slim. The best she could hope for was a position as a permanent concubine or a mistress.

Why not his?

With that idea lifting his spirits, Esag strode into Ashegan's residence with a big smile on his face.

"Hello, my lovely intended."

His greeting was met with a frown. "You are late."

8

ANNANI

Six weeks into Khiann's daily tutoring, Annani had learned very little about commerce and a lot about her own sexuality, or as much as was possible to explore with both of them keeping their clothes on.

There was only so much they could allow themselves to do under the protection of the shroud. From time to time people stopped by to talk to them, and there was always a chance a god or goddess would venture into the gardens.

Shrouding did not work on gods, only on immortals and humans.

Frustration had become Annani's constant companion, so much so that she had started snapping at poor Gulan for no good reason. Despicable behavior, since the girl could not retaliate. She was just an easy and available target. Annani felt disgusted with herself for the way she was treating her best friend.

Bottom line, it was time to graduate from Khiann's course on sensuality, or at least move to the next level.

Meaning, she had to find them a private place where they could finally touch each other all over without worrying about getting caught.

The gazebo was no good, and so was her room. The entire palace would know if she invited Khiann into her chamber. Which left only one option.

Enlisting Ekin's help.

If there was any god who would be willing to risk her father's wrath, it was Ekin. As second in command and an invaluable scientist and inventor, Ekin was untouchable, and he knew it. There was nothing Ahn could or would do to him.

Her uncle would also be sympathetic to her cause. Or at least she hoped he would. Ekin was all for free love, but he was also Mortdh's father. Annani still found it hard to believe that he would choose her side over his own son, even if the two were not on speaking terms.

"I am going to talk to my uncle," she told Gulan.

"Do you want to change before you go, my lady?"

Annani glanced down at what she was wearing. Her dress was clean and free of unsightly creases. "Why would I?"

"I thought you would want to wear one of the new ones the seamstress delivered this morning."

Right. Annani always wore her new clothes right away. Except, lately she could not care less about clothing or other adornments. Her head was filled with Khiann.

Except, she should not veer away from her habits lest people become suspicious. Delani had sure been full of questions as she had checked the fit and had made a few adjustments on the spot.

Her suspicions about the woman being one of Mortdh's spies had solidified after the visit. To be fair, though, Annani had been unreasonably anxious lately, suspecting every servant. It could have been all in her head. After all, there was nothing new about Delani's barrage of questions, or her prattle.

"Hand me the yellow one."

"Yes, my lady."

The blue looked nicer on her, but Annani wanted to keep it for her evening meeting with Khiann.

When they reached her uncle's study, Annani motioned for Gulan and her guards to stay outside and entered by herself.

As usual, she found Ekin poring over his large tablet and drawing on it with a stylus.

"What are you working on now?"

"A design for a faster boat." He immediately went into a long explanation about how his new design would improve commerce and how much money it would save the palace.

"Uncle, I did not come here to talk about commerce. Fates know I have had enough of it over the past six weeks."

He smiled. "Is the new tutor working out well?"

Annani felt a blush creep up her cheeks. "Very well indeed."

"I am glad."

Not one to beat around the bush, Annani plunged in. "I need a favor from you."

"Anything." Ekin straightened up, took her elbow, and led her to his chaise. "Tell me what you need, and I shall see what I can do."

Sitting next to her uncle, Annani debated whether she should just tell him what she wanted and why straight up, or talk around it and hope he would understand.

Ekin was bright, and his nature was more similar to hers than that of her parents. He would know what she meant and not make a big fuss about impropriety or some other nonsense like that.

Still, she was a bit embarrassed.

Taking a deep breath, Annani rearranged the folds of her yellow dress. "For the past six weeks, my tutor has conducted the lessons in the gazebo. There are a lot of distractions over there. Birds chirping, small animals scurrying through the undergrowth, and people coming and going and interrupting us constantly. I was wondering if we could have our lessons here. I could learn so much more without all those interruptions."

A big grin split Ekin's face. "I will be happy to assist you, niece. Let me show you a chamber you may use for your studies." He got up and offered her his hand.

"Right through here." Ekin opened one of the doors on the other side of his study. Behind it was a corridor, leading to other chambers in his private wing of the palace.

"I think this one is perfect." He paused in front of one of the doors and pushed it open. "What do you think?"

A large bed took up most of the space in the room. Besides the bed, there was an elegant chaise with a high arm and a privacy partition for dressing. There was no desk or table.

Annani looked up at her uncle. "Is it private?"

"Very, and it has an adjacent washroom." He walked over to the chaise and patted the tall arm. "A lot of interesting studying could be done on this piece of furniture."

Annani blushed. She was a virgin, but that did not mean she did not know what Ekin was implying.

Naughty god.

"What about your servants?"

"Many of my companions require discretion. My staff are not allowed in this wing unless I tell them it is all right to enter and clean it. I dismiss anyone who does not adhere to my instructions. As far as everyone is concerned, you and your tutor will be using my study for your lessons while I am there, chaperoning."

Annani stretched up on her tiptoes and kissed her uncle's cheek. "You are the best, Ekin."

"So I have been told." He winked.

9

KHIANN

"Tell me again, why are we going to Ekin's study?" Khiann asked as Annani led him down the palace's wide corridor.

The sprite was up to something, and he had a feeling it was not studying. Was Ekin on one of his excursions and Annani thought to use his quarters?

A crazy idea, since she was followed everywhere by her guards. The gazebo was outdoors, a public area of the palace, and no one made a fuss about the guards not spending every moment with her there. Only the cook and her assistants knew that they spent every evening in the kitchens, waiting for Annani's cakes to be ready.

A room in Ekin's quarters was a different story.

"As I have explained before, there are too many distractions in the gazebo, and I have a hard time concentrating on your most eloquent lectures. I asked Ekin if we could use his study, and he graciously agreed."

"I see." He did not, but by the barely contained smirk

on Annani's beautiful face, the princess had something interesting planned.

"Here we are." She knocked on the door.

It was immediately opened by Ekin himself, not a servant.

"Good evening, my favorite niece." He bent to kiss Annani's cheek.

"I am your only niece." She entered and motioned for Khiann to follow, then turned around to Gulan and the guards. "Since we will be working on my assignment together with my uncle, you are free to go. Come back in two hours. We have a lot of work to do."

"As you wish, my lady." Gulan looked suspicious but bowed and turned on her heel nonetheless.

The guards looked happy to be dismissed.

"Thank you, my lady," the one on the left said.

"We shall return in two hours," the other one said.

Annani waved a hand. "Take your time. It might take more than two hours."

The guards bowed and followed Gulan down the corridor.

A moment after the door enclosed them in the study, Annani pumped her small fist in the air. "Ekin, you are a genius."

"I know." The god smiled and offered Khiann his hand. "We have met before, Khiann son of Navohn and the lovely Yaeni, but we never clasped hands in friendship."

Disturbed by the god's words, Khiann shook the hand he was offered. "Thank you for welcoming us into your study."

"My pleasure, son."

Ekin had a notorious reputation, and referring to Khiann's mother as lovely might have suggested that the two were more than acquaintances. It was not something a son wanted to contemplate about his mother.

His parents were not a truelove match, but nevertheless, there was plenty of love between them. As far as Khiann knew, neither his father nor his mother had ever strayed. Except, it was not something parents shared with their children. He might have been blissfully unaware.

"Would either of you care to explain what is going on?" he asked.

Ekin raised a brow at Annani. "You did not tell him?"

"I wanted it to be a surprise. Besides, we were not alone for even one moment."

The god grinned, the corners of his eyes crinkling in amusement. Ekin was so ancient that he was actually showing some slight signs of aging. "Let us not waste time then. Follow me, children." He turned around and walked over to one of the doors leading out of his study.

"I am not a child, uncle."

"You will always be a child to me, my lovely niece."

Khiann was relieved. Apparently, Ekin used the term lovely liberally.

It was evident that the two not only liked each other but also shared many characteristics. Hopefully, though, Annani had not inherited her uncle's propensity for seeking variety, just his smarts, and his upbeat personality.

Ekin opened one of the doors lining the corridor of his private wing and motioned for them to enter. "I will see you when I see you. If anyone comes looking for you, I shall shoo them away. Have fun, kids." He winked before closing the door on them.

"Surprise!" Annani wrapped her arms around his neck and pulled him down for a passionate kiss.

Khiann was stunned.

Was Ekin providing cover for them, letting them use one of the bedchambers in his private quarters?

It was inconceivable.

And it was not safe.

"What if one of Ekin's servants finds us here?"

Still holding on to his neck and forcing him to bend almost in two, Annani grinned. "My uncle's reputation is not in vain. He runs his household with the privacy of his partners in mind. His staff are not allowed in this area unless he specifically instructs them to go in and clean it."

"What if this is a trap?" Khiann dislodged her arms so he could straighten up.

Annani waved a hand. "Pfft, Khiann. You are even more paranoid than I am. I trust Ekin."

"Mortdh's father."

"Yes." And to prove it, she tugged on her dress, letting it fall to the floor, and then stepped out of it, wearing nothing other than her glorious skin.

All objections forgotten, Khiann was rendered speechless once again.

During the past six weeks, he had had his hands on every curve of Annani's magnificent body, even on some of her naked skin, but this was the first time he was seeing her without a stitch of clothing on.

Mirth dancing in her eyes, she put a hand on her hip and struck a pose, looking as regal without clothes as she looked in the most elaborate of gowns. "Say something."

He rubbed a hand over his mouth, wiping away the few droplets of venom that had dripped from his fully extended fangs onto his lower lip.

"You are so incredibly beautiful," he said with a slur.

Up until now, Khiann had managed to refrain from biting Annani by the sheer force of his willpower. As a result, for the past six weeks, his venom glands had been permanently swollen. Unlike human males, gods and immortals did not have the luxury of letting off steam by their own hands, or at least not entirely. Biting a pillow just did not do the trick. The venom had to be released into a female's bloodstream.

The problem was that if injected repeatedly, the venom was addictive. Until Annani was certain beyond the shadow of a doubt that she wanted him as her mate, he could not allow himself to get her addicted to him.

He could have used the services of paid partners, but it did not feel right to do so. Khiann wanted only Annani and had decided to abstain until she was ready. Besides, she expected him to stay true to her.

As a result, there was not even a drop of patience left in him. He feared that the moment he had her naked body in his arms, he was going to bite her.

Her eyes hooded with desire, Annani sauntered toward the bed and climbed on top of it. "Now it is your turn to show me this magnificent body of yours. I have been waiting for this moment quite impatiently."

Khiann shook his head.

He was in deep trouble. His fangs wanted inside Annani's neck, and his shaft wanted inside her womanhood. If he removed his breeches, he would attack her before ensuring her readiness.

His only chance of holding off was to leave them on until she was well prepared to receive him.

"Do you remember the deal we have made? You are to follow my commands, not the other way around."

Annani pouted. "I remember."

10

ANNANI

That was disappointing. Annani had been looking forward to seeing Khiann in all his magnificence just as much as she had been craving their joining.

"But why not? I want to see you."

"You will, just not all of me right away. Patience, my love. I promise you will see everything before we leave this room." He reached for the bottom of his tunic and pulled it over his head.

Wow, Khiann was perfection. Annani's mouth watered at the sight of his muscular chest and arms.

All gods had handsome bodies and beautiful faces, but most of them led sedentary lives and did not develop big bulging muscles like Khiann's.

"How did you get to be so big?"

He glanced down at the huge erection tenting his breeches. "This is your doing." He lifted a pair of worried eyes. "I hope it does not scare you."

Typical male, thinking everything was about his manhood.

Rolling her eyes, Annani waved a hand. "I will admit your size is somewhat intimidating, but my question referred to your muscles, not your erection."

"Oh." He sounded disappointed.

"Do not get me wrong, it is very impressive," she added quickly. "But I expected its size to be proportionate to your height. What I did not expect were all those yummy muscles."

A small smirk lifted one corner of Khiann's mouth, making him look comical given that his fangs were fully extended. It was like watching a tiger smile. "I practice fencing with Esag daily. I need to be able to defend myself and my entourage on the caravan routes. The roads are infested with bandits."

It should have worried her that Khiann found it necessary to learn fighting skills to fend off potential attacks on his trading expeditions. Instead, it only enhanced his appeal in her eyes. There was something very alluring about a capable warrior. As a god, Khiann had abilities that would most likely make actual hand to hand combat unnecessary. Still, the fact that he knew how to wield a sword excited her.

As the spike in her desire reached Khiann's nostrils, the glow in his eyes intensified. He sucked in a breath and advanced on her, his powerful body moving with the grace and fluidity of a predator, his fangs and intense eyes making him look feral.

Magnificent god.

Oddly, Annani felt no trepidation despite the sight of his glowing eyes, his fully elongated fearsome fangs, and the erection tenting his breeches, not to mention the horror tales of how difficult and painful the first time was for a female. Thankfully, goddesses did not have a maidenhead like human and immortal females, so there would be no tearing and no blood involved, except maybe for where he was going to bite her.

According to Delani and Nai, though, it was the best part of the joining. A god's venom was a powerful aphrodisiac and produced the best orgasms. Annani could not wait to experience Khiann's bite even if a little pain was involved, or a lot.

She was not worried about that part of the joining. The size of his erection, however, was another story. He was a big male, while she was a tiny female. Even without the need to breach a barrier, the fit was not going to be comfortable.

Khiann caught her staring at the tent in his pants. "Do not be afraid, my beautiful flower." He leaned over her, his eyes roaming over every curve before he kissed her lips. "By the time I am done preparing you, you will be so soaking wet that I will glide inside you effortlessly."

Her male was delusional. It was going to hurt. But she could deal with that. After all, Delani had reassured her that only the first couple of times were painful, hastening to add that she would feel pleasure as well. Supposedly, by the third time, the pain would be gone, and only the pleasure would remain.

"I am not afraid of pain. If babies can pass through my channel, so can your manhood. I trust you to make it good for me in the end."

She wrapped her arms around his neck and brought

him down to lie on top of her. The feel of his big body blanketing hers was heavenly. Annani had waited a long time to experience this type of closeness, and it was even better than she had imagined.

As he lifted his torso and braced on his forearms, Khiann gazed at her with love in his glowing eyes. "I cherish your trust. It is the most precious gift you can give me."

"More precious than my virginity?"

"Much more. Although I cherish that too."

She liked his answer a lot. Khiann was right to value her trust over her virginity. It was much harder to give away.

Dipping his head, he slanted his lips over hers, gently, careful not to nick her with his fangs as he slipped his tongue into her mouth. His gentleness did not last long, though. After a few swipes against her tongue, he deepened the kiss, thrusting into her mouth, claiming it as thoroughly as if it were a prelude to another taking.

By the time Khiann lifted his head and moved to his side, Annani's body was quivering with need.

Gazing at her puckered nipples with heated eyes, he murmured, "Beautiful."

As he smoothed his palm over her hip and then continued up to the valley of her narrow waist, feathering his fingers over her heaving ribcage, Annani held her breath. When his hand finally made contact with her breast, she released it with an audible whoosh and then moaned as he dipped his head and licked her straining nipple.

Yes, that was precisely what she needed.

Arching her back, Annani demanded more than the lazy swipes of his tongue. Not one to deny her, not for long anyway, Khiann gently took the hard peak between his lips and suckled on it, at the same time rolling the other one between his fingers.

Annani was on fire, so turned on that she could have climaxed just from that, or rather from the anticipation of his next move. During their so-called lessons, he had brought her to several shattering orgasms just by masterfully fondling her breasts.

Fates, he had given her so much pleasure over the six weeks of his courtship. Annani could not wait to do the same in return. Except, she had to stick to the deal she had made and follow his lead until their third joining.

It would be amazing to finally have her hands and her mouth on him. Everywhere. For some reason, though, Khiann had denied her the pleasure of touching his manhood. Hopefully, her curiosity would be sated tonight.

As his suckling turned more forceful, she braced for what was coming next, almost crying in relief when his fingers closed around her other nipple and pinched. It was the oddest thing, but she craved the little zings of pain. They enhanced her pleasure, bringing her to a faster orgasm than all of his gentle touches put together.

"Yes!" she mewled. "More!"

Khiann pinched harder while applying pressure to her other nipple with his blunt front teeth.

The first time he had done it in the gazebo, she had feared that he might nick her with his sharp fangs, but somehow he had managed not to. Not even once.

His admirable self-control and the care he took with

her endeared him to Annani even more. It must have been so hard for him to give and give without getting any relief in return. But he had insisted on focusing entirely on her and her pleasure, learning her, teaching her, developing her trust in him.

What she had learned was that he would never hurt her, intentionally or unintentionally, which allowed her to enjoy the things he did to her without even a shadow of trepidation.

As the pressure increased, the coil inside her tightened until she was sure it would snap at any moment, but then Khiann released the pressure, soothing one nipple with gentle licks of his tongue and the other with his warm palm.

"Why did you stop? I was so close."

"Patience, precious. Trust me."

The magic words had the desired effect on her, doing away with her frustration. Khiann knew best how to wring the most pleasure out of her. He had proven it many times over.

With a sigh, she relaxed her body, letting it sink into the comfortable bed as Khiann's palm smoothed over her rib cage and started a reverse journey down her belly to her heated sex.

When he cupped her there, Annani's eyes rolled back in her head.

"Spread your thighs for me, love."

She did, letting her legs fall wide and giving him all the access he wanted. He had touched her down below before, bringing her to an orgasm by gently rubbing the apex of her femininity, but he had not penetrated her with his fingers yet. Annani was sure that his long digits would feel a thousand times better than her own tiny ones.

As he teased her wet lower lips, his touch was so featherlight at first that it felt ticklish. When she squirmed a little, letting him know she was growing impatient, his fingers applied a little more pressure, becoming more and more demanding with each sweep.

It was better but not enough. "Please, Khiann. I need more."

Leaning over her, he kissed her at the same time as he started to work his finger inside her.

Finally.

She had been right to think that Khiann's fingers would feel much better than her own, but she had not anticipated that he would have difficulty inserting even one. His single digit was thicker than two of hers, which was the most she had ever done on her own while imagining it was his hand and not hers.

It was worrisome. This was not the easy glide he had promised her, and that was only one finger, not his thick manhood.

But as he kept gently thrusting into her, slowly, his tongue working her mouth in sync with his finger, she relaxed, and her tight sheath started loosening. With her pleasure climbing, more and more lubricant coated Khiann's gentle finger, and when he withdrew and returned with two, she moaned as the new sensation of fullness overwhelmed her.

In a good way.

"Come for me, my beautiful flower," Khiann whispered in her ear as he pressed the heel of his palm against the center of her pleasure.

With a cry, she let the tight coil inside her spring free.

11

KHIANN

His princess was magnificent, and even more so when in the throes of passion.

With a heart overflowing with love, Khiann hugged Annani to him, enveloping her body with his. The urge to bite was still there, but worry stifled the need. She was so small that it had been difficult to work even one finger into her, he had gotten her wet enough to add another, but two of his fingers were not nearly as thick as his shaft.

He had a feeling that tonight would not end in a joining, which would greatly disappoint Annani.

"That was incredible," she mumbled into his chest.

"Yes, it was." He kissed her forehead.

She lifted her head and smiled. "If your fingers brought me so much pleasure, I can only imagine how amazing our joining will feel."

It pained him to do so, but he had to deny her. Annani's first time would set the tone for the rest of her eternal life, and he did not want it to be filled with pain and tears. "It would have to wait for the next time. You are too tight. I need to prepare you better."

"Ugh, Khiann. I love you, and I know I made a deal with you, but you are too cautious with me. I am a goddess. Even if it hurts at first, my body will heal immediately and adjust. I do not want to wait another day." She glanced at his straining manhood. "Besides, I do not think you can wait any longer either."

As she reached for him, he did not stop her this time. A male could withstand only so much.

Sucking in a breath, he braced for the first contact with her small hand, and as she cupped him over his breeches, his hips surged up involuntarily. "You are killing me."

"I am not. You are a god." Annani smirked, letting go of him only to reach inside his pants and palm his naked flesh.

Growling like a beast, he gritted his teeth, which did not work well while sporting fully elongated fangs. "Annani," he hissed as he thrust into her soft palm again.

"So smooth," she breathed. "And so warm. I bet it will feel incredible. Put it in me, Khiann."

Damnation. He was going to come in her hand. Maybe he should. It would certainly relieve the incredible pressure threatening to obliterate his restraint, and he could take his time with her.

"Wow, you are growing even harder. I did not think it was possible. Does it hurt?" She lifted her eyes to his face.

"Keep it up for a few more seconds, and I will climax." He closed his hand over her nape and gave another hard thrust.

"Oh." She let go.

"I did not say it to stop you."

Her eyes widened. "You want me to continue?"

"Yes."

She looked down at his shaft and licked her lips.

Fates, was she going to put her mouth on him?

"Are you going to bite me when you climax?" she asked.

"Do you want me to?"

"Yes," she whispered. "I want it very much."

It would not be the same as biting Annani while he was inside her, which provided the most pleasure for a male, and also for an experienced female, but there was one huge advantage to doing it like that. With his venom working its magic on her body, there would be no pain for her when he penetrated her. After all, a god did not need recovery time. He would be hard and ready immediately after coming in her hand.

Khiann pushed his breeches down, kicking them the rest of the way off as he cupped Annani's bottom. Grinding against her belly, he hissed through his fangs, "Put your hands on me."

She pushed on his chest. "Lie on your back. I want to look at you."

The deal they had made discarded and forgotten, he did as she commanded, lying on his back with his manhood standing up straight and away from his body.

Annani rose to her knees and gave his long body a thorough look over. "You are male perfection, my Khiann. I will commission a sculpture of your nude body, and it will adorn our mated bedchamber."

"Your hands," he hissed again. Talk about sculptures could wait for a more convenient time.

As she smiled and leaned over him, he groaned, then hissed and closed his eyes as she cupped his straining length with both hands. His eyes popped open with a start when he felt her small tongue flicking the mushroom head. "Fates, Annani."

She licked him again, gathering the small bead of moisture from the tip. "I love your taste." She smacked her lips before licking him again, more thoroughly this time.

Fates, he was not going to last. "I am a hair away from erupting. Are you sure about this?"

Annani's eyes were hooded with desire. "Yes, my love. I want to bring you to a climax like you have done for me so many times."

"Come here." He cupped the back of her neck, bringing her on top of him.

Still holding onto his shaft, she draped herself over his body, her cheek resting on his chest. It felt amazing to hold her, their bodies touching all over, but the height difference meant that he could not kiss her like that. It would not do. He needed to claim her mouth. Pushing back, Khiann sat up and pulled Annani with him.

She had no choice but to straddle him. Her eyes closed, she moaned as her heated core rubbed against his shaft. "It feels so good."

"Yes, it does." He palmed the back of her head and pulled her to his mouth. "Now I can kiss you while you pleasure me with your soft hands."

Her smile was radiant as she palmed his length and

offered him her lips. Her touch was heaven, even though it was that of a novice.

Fingers threaded through her thick hair, holding her in place, he kissed her long and hard, his other hand finding her breast and fondling her nipple.

She moaned, and she writhed, but her up and down movements never faltered, sending his seed shooting up from his shaft.

Holding the back of her head in an iron grip, Khiann tilted it sideways, elongating her neck, and struck with a hiss.

Annani cried out when his fangs broke her skin, tensing for a moment, but as the venom hit her bloodstream, her body slumped, and she collapsed on top of him.

12

ANNANI

As they clung to each other, their bodies sticky from Khiann's climax, Annani felt like she was floating on clouds. The stories she had been told had not done the venom bite justice.

The feeling was indescribable.

She had orgasmed as soon as the initial pain of it had subsided, which must have taken no more than a couple of seconds. But it was about much more than the physical sensations. The connection she felt to Khiann had intensified tenfold, a hundredfold. It was as if every cell in her body wanted to cling to one of his. She never wanted to part with him, not for a second.

Through the euphoric haze, she felt him lifting her up and laying her down on her back, then climbing on top of her. She wrapped her arms around his torso, welcoming his weight.

Khiann was hers for eternity.

His hands threading through her thick hair, he kissed her gently. "I love you, my beautiful flower."

"I love you too. So much so that my heart feels like it is going to burst. Make me yours, Khiann. Join us."

He kissed her again, then reached between their bodies, positioned himself at her entrance, and pushed in, just a little, then stopped.

After climaxing twice, Annani was as slick as she was ever going to get. It should have been easy, but it was not. Thanks to the venom, she felt no pain, only immense pressure.

If she had not known better, she would have feared getting split in half.

Bracing on his forearms, Khiann looked at her with eyes full of passion mingled with worry. "You are still so tight, my love," he slurred. His fangs, which had retracted after he had bitten her, were back to their full length.

Was he going to bite her again?

Fates, she hoped so.

The thought elicited another outpour of lubricant, allowing Khiann to slide a little more of his manhood inside her.

"Keep going. I will stretch for you."

He cupped her cheeks and kissed her again while pressing a little more of himself inside her.

This was not how she imagined their first joining. In her fantasies, Khiann seated himself with one brutal thrust, waited for a moment or two for her to adjust to his girth, and then pounded into her until climaxing with his fangs embedded in her neck.

In reality, it was a much more difficult feat to accomplish, and Khiann was a much more thoughtful and gentle lover than she had anticipated.

Fates, how she loved this male.

Beads of sweat dotting his forehead, Khiann was obviously struggling to maintain control.

Annani lifted her arms and wrapped them around his neck, then closed her eyes and arched her back, forcing a bit more of him inside her. It was an odd sensation having half of her sheath full to bursting and the other empty.

Still a little dazed from the venom's euphoric effect, Annani felt brave. "Push harder," she whispered.

"Patience, my love."

"Please, just do it." She was not sure if it was her impetuous nature talking or the venom, but she had no more patience left.

Annani wanted the joining consummated.

As Khiann lifted his head and looked into her eyes, what he saw must have convinced him that she was adamant about seeing it through.

"Spread wider for me."

She did, going as wide as she could.

He took hold of her hips, his fingers digging into her flesh, and pushed. Hard. Annani cried out, realizing how much restraint he had exercised until now.

Khiann stilled and after a moment started to withdraw, but Annani would have none of that.

She loved him to pieces for being so considerate and selfless, but this joining was happening now. Reaching down, she cupped his buttocks and held him to her with all her strength. "Keep going."

When the stubborn god still did not move, she bit his shoulder. Her fangs might have been tiny and had no venom to discharge, but they could pierce his skin.

As the exquisite taste of Khiann's blood exploded over her tongue, a new outpour of moisture occurred, allowing him to slide back easily to where he had been before.

With a growl, Khiann pushed the rest of the way in, seating himself to the hilt.

Victory.

Finally. She was deliciously filled up, stretched out to her utmost limit, but thanks to Khiann's venom there was no pain, no burning sensation, just a wondrous feeling of oneness.

Releasing his bottom, she tightened her arms around his back and bucked up, spurring him into action.

His eyes gazing lovingly into hers, Khiann pulled almost all the way out, then pushed back in. Slowly, gently, he repeated the move several times. But when she smiled up at him in encouragement and arched up, the last of his restraint snapped.

Now, this was precisely what she had been fantasizing about.

The powerful god on top of her finally realized that she was not going to break and started pounding into her in earnest. Holding onto her hips so she would not slide away from him, his thrusts became frantic, and when his shaft swelled inside her, stretching her beyond what she thought was possible, he threw his head back and roared, then bit her again as he climaxed, wresting another orgasm out of her. Then as the venom hit her system, she orgasmed again, and again.

Exhausted, Annani let herself drift away.

13

KHIANN

A knock on the door awakened Khiann. "Kids, your time is up," Ekin said quietly through the closed door. "It has been more than three hours. I cannot hold people off for much longer. You need to hurry up."

"Give us a few more minutes," Khiann answered in the same low tone.

"I wish I could give you more time, but a few minutes is all I can manage."

"Thank you."

There was a quiet chuckle. "My pleasure."

Annani stirred, pulling the blanket over her and tucking the corner under her chin.

Adorable.

Khiann loved her so much he wanted to pick her up and carry her around with him wherever he went. Being away from her was inconceivable.

He kissed her nose. "You need to get up, love."

"I know." She did not open her eyes.

"Let me carry you to the washroom."

"That would be lovely. Thank you."

He tugged on the blanket. "How are you feeling? Anything hurt?"

"I am feeling wonderful." She opened her eyes and wrapped her arms around his neck. "Nothing hurts."

He lifted her up. "Thank the merciful Fates."

In the washroom, he helped her clean up and then wrapped her in a drying cloth.

Sitting on a stool, she watched him wash, her eyes roaming his body as if she was still hungry for him. Involuntarily, he got hard again.

Annani smiled. "I wish we had time for another round. You know how the saying goes. With the meal comes the appetite."

He lifted her into his arms and carried her back to the bedchamber. "I wish we did not have to part at all. How can I live without you for even one hour?" He lowered her down to the bed and went to retrieve her dress from the floor. "I wish we'd already had our joining ceremony and were free to be together at all times."

Annani sighed as she pulled the dress on. "I wish so too. I will talk with my father about allowing us more time together."

Khiann paused with his tunic in hand. "Are you ready to tell him that I am your one and only?"

"Of course. I was ready six weeks ago." She waved a hand. "The courtship phase only confirmed what I knew all along. You are mine, Khiann, and I want to claim you officially."

He went over to where she was sitting and knelt at

her feet. "Let us talk to your father together. I want us to get officially engaged."

Annani chuckled. "Who is impatient now?" She cupped his cheeks and leaned to kiss his lips. "Before we do anything rash, we should talk to Ekin and ask his advice. He will know the best way to proceed."

Khiann still did not feel right about confiding in Ekin, even though the god had made this magical night possible for them. "Maybe we should talk to my father instead. He is one of the oldest gods and has a lot of experience. He also knows your father well. They have been friends since the very beginning."

"We can ask both. Two smart gods are better than one, right?"

There was another knock on the door. "Kids, please hurry up."

"We are coming," Annani called out.

Khiann shrugged his tunic on and offered his hand to Annani. "Come on, love, let us talk to your uncle first."

Holding hands, they walked back to Ekin's study.

They found the god pacing the large space.

"Thank the Fates," he said as he saw them. "I guess congratulations are due, but first you need to go out and calm your maid and your guards. They were worried enough to try and pressure me into allowing them in. While you are at it, I will pour us some wine."

As Annani stepped out and admonished her maid and her guards for pestering Ekin while she was working hard on her report, her uncle took three goblets off the shelf, poured a generous helping of wine into each, and handed one to Khiann.

"All done," Annani said as she closed the door. "I sent them away and told them I have at least another hour of studying to do."

Ekin raised a brow. "You are not done?"

Annani blushed. "Is one ever done?"

Her uncle beamed with pride and patted her shoulder. "You are my blood, that is for sure."

"We need your advice," Khiann said.

"I see." Ekin handed Annani a goblet, then motioned for them to follow him to the chaise.

"So this is it," he said as they were all seated. "You want to make it official."

"Yes," Khiann said.

"You need to talk to Ahn, not me."

"I know that, uncle. What I want from you are pointers. How should we approach him? What should we say?"

His brows drawn tight, Ekin sipped on his wine for a few moments, then turned to Annani. "You should talk to Ahn and your mother first, and then wait for your father to invite Khiann. Ahn will want to ascertain that what you feel for the boy is more than an infatuation. Only after he is convinced of that, will he put Khiann through similar questions to make sure it is the real deal for him as well."

Annani crossed her arms over her chest. "Why can he not take our word for it? We know what we feel for each other is true."

"For his own peace of mind. Ahn is risking war for your happiness, Annani."

PART 4

LOVE'S TRIUMPH

1

MORTDH

As Mortdh read the latest update from his head spy at Ahn's court, his first reaction was disbelief. The second was rage. Crumpling the scroll in his fist, he hurled it against the wall.

"What is it, Father?" Navuh asked as he went to retrieve it.

"Everyone out!" Mortdh bellowed, sending the servants scurrying away.

"Bad news?" Navuh asked as everyone else cleared the chamber.

Mortdh cast a soundproofing shroud before answering. "The whoring daughter of the usurper is making a mockery out of me."

"Annani?"

"Does the usurper have another daughter that he promised to me and is now spreading her legs for someone who is not me?"

"May I?" Navuh asked as he unfurled the scroll.

Mortdh waved a hand. "Go ahead. Burn it when you are done. I do not wish news of my shame to spread."

He had worked long and hard to build up his rule over the northern region. The humans and immortals residing in his territory believed that he was an independent sovereign, and that he did not have to answer to the southern ruler and his precious assembly of gods.

Mortdh was revered as the highest of gods, the king of them all, and by joining with the little slut, it could have even been true.

"Those are only rumors, my lord," Navuh said as he rolled the scroll and tossed it into the fire. "It is not uncommon for young gods and goddesses to have tutors."

Mortdh glared at his son. "Surely you are not so naive as to believe your own words, Navuh. Other than their own children, gods do not tutor other gods. It is a ploy to allow the bastard access to her without alerting me." Mortdh rose to his feet and walked over to the fireplace.

Warming his hands, he watched the parchment smolder, much like the fury inside him. His father had been cheated out of his rightful place as head of the gods, and Mortdh was determined to correct that wrong. Not for Ekin, but for himself.

The next leader of the gods would be the rightful successor.

If not for the stupid matriarchal succession rules, the brilliant and cunning Ekin would have been sitting on the throne, and not his younger and less deserving brother. Mortdh would have been the successor, not the little whore.

So what if Ekin was born to a concubine and Ahn to the official wife?

What difference did it make which cunt they had emerged from?

Ekin was their father's eldest son and therefore should have been king. When he stepped down to pursue his science, which he would no doubt have done sooner rather than later, Mortdh would have taken his place eons ago as the head of the gods, immortals, and humans everywhere.

Once he seized the throne, he was going to do away with any custom or tradition that gave cunts power. Starting with the right of consent. They were breeders, nothing more, and as such they should be treated like livestock to be sold and bought on the market. In fact, he was going to do away with the gods' entire code of law. There would be no more need for the big or small assembly because there would be no more voting on anything.

Mortdh was going to lord supreme over them all, and they were going to accept him as an absolute ruler because he knew what was best for everyone.

The humans and immortals residing in his territory worshiped him not out of fear, but out of gratitude.

He was good to them.

Unlike the other gods, who sat on their asses all day and expected humans to provide for them, Mortdh provided for his people.

His region was prospering thanks to the lucrative cedar tree exports, and he was funneling the profits to his people by hiring them to serve in his ever-growing army and to build his temple mound.

Unlike his uncle's domain, Mortdh's territory was clear of bandits. After several raiding parties had been dealt with swiftly and harshly, the others moved south where they continued their raids with impunity.

"Even if it is true," Navuh said. "A goddess Annani's age is still very impressionable, and her mind could be changed for her. May I speak freely, Father?"

Mortdh waved his hand impatiently. "That was the idea behind dismissing the servants. Talk."

"Thank you." Navuh took a deep breath and steepled his fingers. "You have not courted Annani. You have not gone to visit her. Perhaps a visit is due. You can dazzle the girl with your good looks and your commanding presence, as well as the many expensive gifts you will bring. You can make her forget all about the new contender for her affections, assuming that there is indeed one and the tutor is not really just a tutor."

"I agree. I have been negligent."

For some reason, it had never occurred to Mortdh that one day Annani would reach the age of majority and might choose another as her mate. Instead of waiting, he should have arrived at Ahn's palace and mated with the girl right on that day.

In his defense, he had not counted on Ahn spoiling the brat to such a degree that she would dare challenge the promise her father had made to Mortdh.

There were rumors that Annani was hotheaded and not the obedient daughter Ahn should have raised, but Mortdh had not extrapolated the possible ramification of his future bride's faulty character. Frankly, over the years since the promise had been made, he had spared her little thought at all.

Except, what if it was not Annani's idea to hire the pretend tutor but Ahn's?

Had his simpering uncle changed his mind, and was he actually instigating a war? It was possible that rumors of Mortdh's growing army had reached him and he wanted to crush Mortdh before he became undefeatable.

That was what Mortdh would have done, but it was unlike his uncle to pursue such violent action. It seemed that after mating Nai, Ahn had started to believe in his own propaganda about the gods being peaceful and benevolent.

His uncle had been a fierce and ruthless leader before joining with the young goddess. When the humans had increased in numbers to the degree that had threatened the gods, he had no qualms about arranging a mass culling.

Even Mortdh would not have gone that far. He would have taken out the leaders, killed a few hundred to scare the rest, and taken control of the situation.

Humans were not much of a threat if one knew how to manage them.

In fact, they were the base of Mortdh's power. Without them, he could not win a war against his brethren. Unlike his uncle, though, he knew how to control humans. All it took to keep their hordes in check was strong leadership. Without it, humans were like sheep—unpredictable and easily excitable. In the hands of a capable shepherd, however, they were a force to reckon with.

The problem was that his army was not ready yet. Until he amassed a strong enough force to win a war against Ahn and the other gods, he was going to stall by exhausting every political maneuver available to him.

"Gifts are a good idea. Assemble a caravan. Fill it with jewelry, rare fabrics, exotic slaves, and whatever else you may deem appropriate. I am putting you in charge of delivering everything and dazzling the little whore."

"As you wish, Father. How soon do you want it done?"

"Make it so you can leave in three days."

"As you command, Father." Navuh bowed. "Will you be flying ahead of the caravan?"

Navuh was still young and did not understand that perception was everything. "No, my son. If the gifts do the trick, I will not come at all. I do not want to waste my time on her. I am sending you with my elite squadron of immortal warriors and wagons piled with goods." He lifted his hands. "It will send a clear message—a sword in one hand, and a pomegranate in the other. I trust your judgment. Assess the situation, and if you decide that my presence is necessary, inform me, and I will fly over to join you."

Navuh bowed again. "I bask in the light of your wisdom, Father."

2

ANNANI

"You wished to see me, Mother?" Annani asked as she entered her parents' private quarters.

It had been a long time since she had been allowed in there. Most of the mother-daughter meetings were conducted either in Nai's reception room or the throne room.

It was highly unusual for Annani to be invited to the royal couple's private chamber.

"Yes, indeed." Nai turned to her maids and Gulan. "I wish to speak with my daughter in private. Everyone else, please leave."

"As you wish, my lady." Her mother's head maid bowed and ushered the others out.

"Come sit with me," Nai commanded as the door closed behind the maids.

Should she worry? What was it all about? Was her mother going to subject her to another lecture on why she should not join with Khiann yet?

Annani stifled a smile. It was a little too late for that.

Thank the Fates, the scent of incense permeated the chamber. Without it, there would have been no way for Annani to mask her feelings of happiness from her mother. The heavy perfume she had doused herself with could only do so much.

"I heard that you and Khiann used Ekin's workspace for your lesson yesterday, and that you have spent many hours on your report." Nai raised one perfectly arched brow.

"Yes."

"Could I see that report?"

Camel droppings, there was no report. Annani had scribbled a few notes, but it was not what three hours of work should have produced.

"It is not finished. I still have a lot of work to do on it until it is ready for presentation."

Nai laughed. "What do you take me for, child, a fool? I know perfectly well what you and Khiann did yesterday."

Damnation. Should she continue to pretend? What if her mother had informants who had spied on them last night?

It was not a remote possibility. It was a certainty.

One of Nai's earliest lessons to her daughter was about a ruler's need to have eyes and ears everywhere to inform him or her of what was going on around them.

Still, Annani could always answer a question with another question and not commit to anything. It was one of the things she had learned from listening to what went on in the throne room. "What do you think we did, Mother?"

Nai patted her knee. "I know Ekin. Someone who refers to himself as the god of free love and fornication is not much of a chaperone."

"He is not?"

"Oh, stop the innocent act, Annani. You are not fooling me. Ekin covered for you and Khiann while the two of you necked in some dark corner of his quarters."

Annani suppressed the relieved breath she wanted to exhale.

Except, her mother did not miss much. "It was more than necking, was it?"

Annani nodded, letting the smile she had been stifling since morning finally spring free.

Nai chuckled. "That good, eh?"

A blush heating her cheeks, Annani nodded again. "Indescribable," she whispered and took her mother's hands in hers. "I want to join with Khiann as soon as possible. We cannot bear being away from each other for more than a few hours. Can you talk with Father for me?"

"Are you absolutely sure Khiann is your one?"

"Positive. If I cannot have him, I would rather die."

Nai gave her a stern look. "I do not appreciate melodramatics, Annani."

She was not being melodramatic. Without Khiann, there was no purpose to her life, no joy. She would rather perish than live without him. To appease her mother, though, she said, "I will never love another."

"That I can believe. You are too much of a fighter to choose death no matter what, my daughter. Besides, it is a selfish thing even to contemplate."

"If a person finds life too difficult to live, how is it selfish to wish to end the suffering?"

Her mother waved a hand. "In some extreme cases, like a human on his or her deathbed who is suffering intolerable pain, it is acceptable. But it is selfish for a young and capable woman or man to wish it because of heartache. The Fates put you on this earth for a reason. You have a job to do, and you are not free to leave until that job is done."

Annani frowned. "What job?"

"That is for you to find out. It is different for each of us."

Her mother was very confusing. "What is your job?"

"Is it not obvious?"

"Are you talking about ruling along with Father?"

Nai shook her head. "It may seem that way, but no. I was put on this earth for two reasons. The first one was to join with your father and teach him compassion. The second was you. The fortuneteller told me that you are destined for greatness."

Annani huffed. "Since when do you believe in that nonsense, Mother? Fortunetellers will say whatever they think you want to hear, or what some god or immortal thralled them to believe. No one can see the future because it did not happen yet."

Nai nodded. "There are thousands of possible futures, that is true. But I do believe that some humans and immortals have a real gift for feeling which one will come to pass."

"Perhaps," Annani agreed just to end the whole discussion about seers. In her opinion, the visions some humans and immortals had were the product of godly pranks, some of them quite malicious. None of the gods ever claimed to be able to see the future. Anyone making such a claim would have been ridiculed.

"You just need to open your mind to the possibility, child. We are thought of as gods by those inferior to us, but that does not make us all-knowing."

"I promise to dedicate some serious thought to it, Mother." Not really.

Nai sighed as if knowing that Annani had no such intention. "I will talk with your father and tell him that you have made up your mind. He will probably want to have another talk with Khiann."

3

KHIANN

As Khiann got ready for his workday, he thanked the Fates for his father's early return. Navohn had not been due back for at least two more days, but favorable weather conditions had allowed the caravan to traverse the distance faster.

According to his father, the winds had been mellow, and the heat had been unusually mild for the season. Khiann had a suspicion that the Fates had something to do with it.

A strange thought for a skeptic like him.

Except, it was hard to argue against their existence when recent events implied otherwise. A mere two moon cycles ago he could not have dreamed of Annani ever being his. The princess had been as unapproachable as the moon itself.

The Fates had been exceptionally kind to him.

The question was why.

Those who believed in them wholeheartedly claimed that they bestowed gifts on those who had sacrificed a lot for others or those who had endured terrible hardships.

Khiann had done neither.

He had been blessed with loving parents and good friends and had not experienced even the slightest of hardships, unless the six torturous weeks of abstinence could count as such. He had definitely suffered, but it had been his choice to dedicate the courtship period to Annani and her pleasure and not ask for anything in return. It had also been his decision not to slake his needs elsewhere.

It had not been easy, but he was quite proud of himself for accomplishing a feat not many male gods or even immortals were capable of. That did not mean, though, that the Fates would consider it a sacrifice. It had not been selfless. They would not reward him for something he had done for his own benefit, whether it was Annani's introduction to the world of carnal pleasures or his own ego.

It worried him. If he had not earned his boon, it was believed that the Fates would demand payment at a later time, and that the payment would be equivalent in value to what they had bestowed.

A payment for love as great as Annani's and his could equal the world's destruction, which was a real possibility if Mortdh could not be appeased.

Still, despite the constant churning in his gut, Khiann would have not changed anything.

Upon entering the kitchen, he found his parents finishing their breakfast.

"Good morning, Mother, Father." He dipped his head before joining them at the table.

"Good morning, Khiann." His mother's smile looked relaxed and natural, which was a welcome change after weeks of seeing her worry and brood. She did not do well in his father's absence.

The thing was, Navohn loved to travel. This was what had prompted him to become a merchant in the first place. But for Yaeni's sake, he should have stayed home more often and let someone else lead the trading expeditions.

Except, if he did that, Khiann would have to take his place, which was the plan until Annani had entered the picture. Now, the last thing Khiann wanted to do was to be without her for weeks at a time.

Mere hours of separation were difficult to endure. Every moment away from his love was painful.

Perhaps they could train Esag to take his place. His squire would be overjoyed to travel extensively and have a legitimate reason to be away from his cantankerous intended.

"Would you like something to eat?" the cook asked.

"Yes, please."

Khiann turned to his father. "Are you all rested?"

Since Navohn had returned late last evening, and after a quick greeting had retired to his mated bedchamber, they had not had the opportunity to talk yet.

"It is good to be home."

"How did your expedition go?"

"Exceedingly well. I have found unimaginable treasures. Come to my office after you are done eating, and I will show you."

Khiann guzzled down the mug of water the cook

had put in front of him, stuffed a piece of bread in his mouth and chewed it in record time. "I am done. Let us go."

Navohn laughed. "I see that you are impatient. And that is even before I hinted at the nature of my marvelous acquisitions." He rose to his feet and leaned to kiss Yaeni. "I will join you for lunch, my love."

"I need to talk to you," Khiann said as they stepped into his father's office. Even after working there for almost two moon cycles, Khiann still could not think of it as theirs or his. It would always be his father's office.

"I am sure you do." Navohn closed the door and cast a soundproofing shroud over the space. "Tell me the news."

"The courtship went well. Annani and I are ready to announce our engagement. She already talked with her mother who in turn talked to Ahn. He wants to see me the day after tomorrow."

Navohn sat on one of the chairs facing his desk and motioned for Khiann to take the other. "Then it is fortunate that I came home early."

"Indeed. I was worried that I would have to talk to Ahn without the benefit of your advice. The Fates were kind to me."

"More than you know, my boy." Navohn smirked.

"What do you mean?"

"The treasure I have found. The moment I laid eyes on them I knew they would be the perfect engagement gift for your princess. Even Mortdh with all his riches could not offer anything comparable. He would have to concede defeat, regardless of Annani's right to choose. You will present your suit with an offer he cannot beat."

Khiann frowned. "Them? Do not tell me you are referring to slaves. Annani abhors slavery."

His father's grin widened. "Then she is going to doubly appreciate this gift."

"What is it?"

Navohn pushed to his feet. "Come, and I will show you."

As he followed his father to the stables, Khiann tried to guess what Navohn was going to show him. Perhaps he had acquired some exotic animals, or maybe a rare breed of horses. Both would be considered an adequate gift, but he doubted Annani would be interested in either.

His princess did not show much interest in animals, and she favored more elegant modes of transportation than horses. Annani either traveled by carriage or used her flying vehicle, one of the few in the gods' possession that were still functional. Most of the rockets and airboats were either broken or missing parts, and since the boat of a million years had departed eons ago, no effort had been made to fix them.

Besides, if anyone knew how to repair the flying machines, it was Ekin, who knew everything there was to know about the gods' technology, but he showed no interest in doing so.

Who knew, perhaps he preferred the gods to be earthbound. Without the flying boats, the gods' fate was tied to that of humans and immortals. There would never be another flood to cull the human population.

As they walked into the furthest stable, Khiann saw seven squat men sitting in a row and sorting through piles of semiprecious stones, separating them by color and size.

Common semiprecious stones? That could not have been the extraordinary gift his father had been referring to. There was nothing special about them. Mountains of those colorful rocks would be needed to impress the heir to the throne.

"Is that it, Father?"

"Are they not extraordinary?" Navohn asked.

"My apologies, but I do not see what is special about these semiprecious stones."

Navohn laughed. "Not the rocks, Khiann, the Odus." He waved his hand at the men.

Maybe his father had spent too much time in the scorching sun, and it had affected his brain. "Slaves? I already told you that Annani is against slavery."

"Even when the slaves are not people but machines?"

Taking a few steps, Khiann got closer and peered at the men, then sniffed. The lingering scent of horses had initially obscured the metallic scent coming off the seven workers, but now that Khiann was paying attention, it was unmistakable. Under the layer of skin and flesh was metal. A lot of it.

Rubbing a hand over his jaw, he looked at his father. "I have never heard of mechanical men."

"Bio-mechanical servants were quite common on our mother world. Ahn and Ekin would know what these are, and they would also realize their incredible value. The technology of creating them was banned. These seven are the only ones in existence. They are irreplaceable and therefore priceless."

4

GULAN

"Ouch," Annani cried out as a strand of her hair got caught on Gulan's bracelet."

"I am so sorry, my lady." Gulan held the strand with the fingers of one hand while gently pulling it out from in between the bracelet's links with the other. "I should remove my jewelry while styling your hair." She took off the bracelet and put it on Annani's vanity table, then resumed her work on her lady's elaborate up-do.

She wondered why Annani even bothered. From experience, Gulan knew that no trace of her hard work would remain after Khiann's visit. Annani's hair would get all tussled and messy from their lovemaking.

It was no longer a secret. By now, everyone knew about her lady's new suitor.

If not for Mortdh, to whom she was still officially promised, and the fact that she was supposed to remain faithful to him, no one would have made a big fuss about the princess taking a lover. After all, she was of age and was allowed to do as she pleased.

In fact, most of their former classmates were either getting into relationships or finalizing them with engagements or joining ceremonies. Gulan had been to quite a few lately.

Her friends were starting their adult lives while she was stuck in place with no prospects in sight.

Unless she counted Esag, which she did not.

It was not as if he was courting her or anything. He was just teaching her to fight. The hints and inappropriate remarks he threw at her from time to time were meaningless.

On Esag's part, it was just mindless flirting, but it was so much more on hers.

She had learned to hide it better, though. After that first time she had run off on him, Gulan had forced herself to exercise better control of her emotions, or rather the way she let them manifest.

She was not going to make a fool of herself again.

Pinning the last strand of red hair on top of the pile she had made, Gulan stepped back and admired her work in the mirror. "Is it to your satisfaction, my lady?" she asked.

"It is beautiful, like all of your creations." Annani patted the mountain of hair and rose to her feet. "I am ready. Are you?"

Gulan put the bracelet back on. "I am now."

Annani eyed the piece of jewelry. "Are you going to practice fighting with that on?"

"No, I will take it off before we start. I do not want to accidentally hurt Esag with it."

She was getting better, which meant that when their sessions were over, Esag often sported bruises. He did not complain. On the contrary, he was so proud and happy every time she managed to land a blow, that Gulan did not feel like she had to hold anything back.

After leaving Annani in the reception chamber her parents had allocated to her meetings with Khiann, or their love room as Annani referred to it, Gulan headed to the palace gardens.

While Annani and Khiann engaged in one form of physical activity, Gulan and Esag engaged in another. It was a less pleasant one, but satisfying in its own way.

"Hi, Gulan," Esag greeted her as she neared the clearing that they had appropriated for their training.

"Hi, yourself. Ready to get beaten?"

"By you, always." He winked.

Here he goes again with his flirting.

After she had run off when he had called her beautiful, Esag had been trying to refrain from flirtatious comments. Except, it seemed like he could not help himself.

It was in his nature. Esag probably flirted with every female he encountered.

Gulan would be a fool to entertain hopes for anything more, especially after Annani's forewarning. Her lady had advised her to ignore Esag and his many charms because he was promised to another.

Except promises of that nature could be broken, as Annani herself was proving, and Gulan could not extinguish the tiny spark of hope in her heart.

What if Esag fell in love with her and broke off his engagement?

Do not be a fool. You are not a beautiful princess, and no one is going to break their promises for you.

"What are you waiting for?" Esag taunted from several feet away. "I do not have all day."

Gulan attacked.

She was freakishly strong, but Esag had years of hard practice on her and the muscles to show for it. He overpowered her in no time, throwing her down to the ground and straddling her. When she tried to grab his hair and pull him off her, he caught her hands and pinned them over her head.

Gulan bucked up, using all of her considerable strength, but Esag held on tight, pressing down even harder.

To her utter bewilderment, she found the submissive pose oddly titillating. Disturbed and embarrassed, Gulan resumed her struggles in an attempt to divert Esag's attention from her sudden and most inappropriate arousal.

Maybe her desperation might produce a strong enough scent to mask the other subtler one.

Several futile moments later, Gulan ceased her efforts and went limp. "I concede defeat. You win. Now, get off me."

"Not so fast."

With no fight left in her, she became aware of Esag's response to her. His eyes were glowing, his fangs were elongating, and she could feel his erection hardening through his breeches. Apparently, he found the pose as arousing as she did.

It made the situation even worse.

Gulan bucked up again. "Get off me, Esag!"

"I want a kiss."

Her breath hitched. Gulan had never been kissed.

But if she allowed Esag to kiss her, the last of the defenses she had built around her heart would no doubt crumble.

She should not say yes to the kiss. Esag did not want her, not really. He was just playing with her. When the time came for him to join with his intended, Gulan's heart would shatter.

She would never be able to pick up the pieces and glue them back together.

And yet, she wanted that kiss more than anything.

Maybe it was her only chance to be kissed by an attractive male, and she might end up forever regretting missing that chance.

When she did not answer, he leaned over her, his lips hovering so close to hers that she could feel the heat from his mouth.

"Last chance to say no, Gulan," he whispered.

When she said nothing at all, he closed the rest of the distance and kissed her.

5

KHIANN

A scroll in his hand, Esag walked into the office. "The summons from the palace arrived," he announced.

"Just in time." Khiann released a breath. A day earlier would have been too soon, and a day later would have been a day too long to wait.

As Esag placed it in his hand, he broke the royal seal without giving it a second glance. Normally, Khiann would have paused to admire the artwork that went into it, but not today.

"It is a formal invitation," he said as he finished reading it. "I am to arrive with my parents and present my official suit."

"When?" Navohn asked.

"Tomorrow evening, right after sunset."

His father grinned. "I guess it is time to get the Odus cleaned up and dress them in fine garments."

The seven were still in the stables, working on sifting through the stones. Apparently, they did not require sleep and could eat almost anything, converting it into energy that animated their mechanical inner workings.

Esag scratched the beard he was starting to grow per his intended's request. Ashegan thought he would look more distinguished with it. "I do not understand how come no one knew about the Odus. I would think a marvel like that would not easily be forgotten and abandoned."

Khiann and his father exchanged glances.

Esag had not been privy to their talks about the gods' history. Other than the original group of gods and very few of their descendants, no one knew the truth about their violent past. It was of vital importance for the humans and their hybrid progeny, the immortals, to believe that the gods were benevolent, peaceful people.

"They were lost," Navohn said. "I found them quite by chance."

"Were they enslaved by humans?" Esag asked.

"No, they would not serve anyone who is not a god, not unless their master told them to do so. They wandered searching for their true masters, offering their services for food and clothing. When they saw me, they recognized who and what I was and followed me, claiming me as their master. Until I transfer ownership to the princess, they will answer only to me."

"I wonder what happened to their original owner," Esag said.

Navohn lifted his hands in the air. "Who knows? There might have been a sandstorm or an earthquake, and they got separated. Their master might still be buried somewhere in the desert, waiting for someone to revive him. A god or an immortal could survive indefinitely in stasis."

The explanation might have satisfied someone not as smart as Esag. "I was under the impression that they can talk. Perhaps they can tell you what happened to their master?"

"I thought the same thing. It seems, however, that their memories were wiped. I do not know if it was done deliberately or if it was a malfunction, but the result is the same. The Odus do not know who they are, where they came from, or who their original master was."

"That is a shame," Esag said. "Should I take them to get washed?"

"Yes, please. And make sure they wash their hair as well. Think of the Odus as small children. They need to be told exactly what to do and how."

"Got it." Esag bowed and turned on his heel.

Khiann waited a few moments before casting a sound barrier around the office. "Did you wipe their memories?"

"No, I was telling the truth about that."

"I still do not understand how they got here. You said their kind was destroyed."

Navohn sighed and leaned back in his chair. "What I said was that after they had been misused for combat in the big war, their making had been prohibited, the technology to build them had been destroyed, and the Odus had been disposed of."

"What is the difference between destroying and disposing of them?"

"The Odus are indestructible. To get rid of them,

they were ejected into space. I suspect that whoever owned these seven did not have the heart to dispose of them that way and sent them to a habitable planet on purpose."

"You want to tell me that there are thousands of them floating in space?"

"If the vessels housing them still hold, then yes."

"But they need to eat and breathe to maintain their biological parts."

"I am not a scientist, but I guess they can go into stasis the same way we do, and survive eons. We can ask Ekin, he should know."

Khiann raked his fingers through his hair. "But if at some point in time they were used for warfare, are they not dangerous? I do not want to give Annani a potentially deadly gift."

"It is all in the programming. The Odus do what their master tells them to do. In fact, they can be programmed to protect her. The princess will be much safer with these seven guarding her at all times. Another bonus is that they will never reveal any of her secrets either. They are the perfect servants."

"If that is so, maybe we should keep one or two for ourselves."

Navohn shook his head. "Even though Ahn considers me a friend, he will not allow such dangerous technology to remain in my hands. With Annani as their mistress, he has nothing to worry about. Unless, of course, she decides to turn on him, but I do not think he has anything to be concerned about in that regard."

6

AHN

As he paced the throne room, Ahn debated the wisdom of his decision to ask Areana to take Annani's place as Mortdh's intended.

There was no upside to it other than the slight chance of averting war by giving Mortdh a way to save face.

The guilt was eating at him.

He was saving one daughter by sacrificing the other. The difference was that he was offering Areana a choice. He had not offered it to Annani, which in retrospect was one of the biggest mistakes he had ever made, and there had been plenty.

Ahn had ruled for a long time, and he was not infallible. It was true that most of the hard decisions he had taken had been voted on by the big assembly, but that did not absolve him of responsibility. He had the power to veto any decision he did not approve of. But in the name of equality and in the spirit of the laws he and the other founders had put in place, Ahn had never vetoed a unanimous vote.

Still, some of the decisions that Ahn regretted had been made by him and him alone. When it came to the safety of his people, the assembly's vote was not needed, and the same was true when it came to his own family.

The thing was, Ahn had always chosen the good of his people over everything and everyone else, and that included his beloved daughter.

"Should I stay for your meeting with Areana?" Nai asked.

He shook his head. "She would be intimidated by your presence."

"I understand." Nai came up to him and wrapped her arms around his neck, pulling him down to her. "I know it is not easy for you, my love." She kissed him briefly before sauntering out of the room.

Ahn sighed. Nai always tried to see the best in him, giving him much more credit than he deserved.

He did not feel for Areana even a fraction of what he felt for Annani. His older daughter was nothing like her half-sister. Where Annani was strong and decisive, Areana was timid and weak.

Truth be told, he found it embarrassing to have produced such an inferior offspring. How could the most powerful god beget one of the weakest?

Unfortunately, it had been proven beyond a shadow of a doubt that Areana was his. As the daughter of a mistress, she had not been raised in the palace, and Ahn had made no effort to get to know her. After her birth, Areana's mother had joined with another god who had acted as a father to her.

He was still pacing when a servant announced Areana's arrival.

"Let her in," he told the immortal.

She bowed upon entering. "Good evening, my lord."

"Good evening, daughter." He put his hands on her shoulders and kissed her on one cheek and then the other. It was a proper fatherly greeting, but it lacked the appropriate emotion.

At least she was beautiful. Mortdh could not complain about her not being pleasing to the eye. And she was sad, deeply so. Which was not surprising since she had lost her fated mate. One did not recover from a tragedy like that.

"Thank you for coming," he said as he led her to a chair.

"You have summoned me. Of course I came."

"Wine?" he asked as he poured himself a goblet.

"Yes, please. Thank you."

She had a pleasant voice, even sweet.

"You are probably wondering why I asked you here." He handed her a full goblet.

"Yes, I am," Areana nodded.

In fact, she kept nodding throughout his long explanation about what he wanted from her and why.

"It is entirely up to you, Areana. Do not feel as if you have any obligation to agree, or that you will disappoint me if you do not. I will find another way to appease Mortdh."

As she sipped her wine for several long moments, he was glad she was giving it serious thought.

Areana put the goblet down on the low table and clasped her hands in front of her. "Since my love was murdered, my life has been meaningless, and it does not matter if I am miserable here or at Mortdh's stronghold. He has so many concubines and mistresses that he will probably leave me alone. Knowing that I helped Annani will give meaning to my empty life. But I am not sure about the spying part. I am not brave, my lord. In fact, I am a coward. If I were brave, I would have ended my life as soon as I lost the reason to keep on living." She lowered her eyes.

Damnation. If his heart were not so black, it would have been weeping for Areana. But after thousands of years of ruling, Ahn was inured to misery as well as guilt. Without Nai in the room, he did not even feel the need to pretend compassion.

"I am not asking you to actively spy on him. Just observe what is going on in his court, and when you come home for a visit, which I am going to insist on as part of your joining, you will report to me what you have observed."

Areana lifted her sad, yet intelligent eyes to him. "Mortdh will expect that of me. I am sure no secrets would be revealed while I am around."

"Yes and no. First of all, he cannot silence everyone in court, and people like to talk. The service staff know everything. If you befriend them, you will know more than the best of spies. In fact, you are perfect for that. As a goddess of limited powers and mellow personality, you will not intimidate them. They will feel free to share gossip with you."

"I heard he uses mostly slaves."

Ahn waved a dismissive hand. "Slaves, servants, it

does not make a difference. People are people regardless of their station, and they like to talk."

7

KHIANN

"Stop right there!" one of the soldiers guarding the palace's front doors ordered. "We were told to accompany Master Khiann and his parents to the reception hall. These men need to stay behind." He pointed at the Odus.

"They are a gift," Navohn said.

The soldier arched a brow. "Slaves?"

"A very special kind," Navohn answered with a smile.

"I need to search them for weapons."

"By all means." His father waved a hand at the seven Odus. "I give you my permission to search them, my good man," he said more for the Odus' benefit than the soldiers'. They needed to hear their master's approval before submitting to the search.

"All clear," the soldier announced when he was done patting down the last one. "You may enter."

Unlike the other time, they were escorted by four armed guards, probably because of the Odus. Or so

Khiann hoped. It would have been most disconcerting if the guards had been sent to escort the three of them.

"Welcome," Ahn said as they were let inside the reception hall.

"Thank you, my lord. And good evening to you and your lovely mate and daughter," Navohn returned the greeting with a bow.

Annani and Nai smiled and dipped their heads.

Khiann bowed, and so did his mother.

"What is that?" Ahn's eyes widened as the Odus followed them inside, accompanied by the guards.

"An engagement present, my lord," Khiann said.

The ruler got to his feet and walked over. "Amazing. I did not think any were left."

"A rare and precious find, worthy of a princess," Navohn offered with a bow.

"You may leave us." Ahn waved at the guards. "These men are harmless."

As the door closed behind the soldiers, Ahn cast a soundproofing shroud. "Where did you find them?"

"It is a long story which I will be glad to tell you over a goblet of wine."

"Of course, where are my manners." Ahn clapped Navohn's shoulder. "Please come in and join us." He pointed to a divan. "What should we do with them while we talk?" The ruler tilted his head toward the seven men standing like statues and awaiting further instructions.

Khiann's father pointed at the room's south wall. "You may sit on the floor over there."

"Yes, master." They bowed in unison and headed to where he had directed them.

As Khiann and his parents sat down across from the royal family, Nai pointed to the low table between the two divans. "Please partake."

The table was loaded with trays of small delicacies, decanters of wine, and pitchers of beer.

"Thank you." Navohn lifted one of the decanters and poured wine into six gold goblets. "Should we toast the joyous occasion?"

Ahn lifted his goblet. "To Annani and Khiann. May their joining be full of love, and fruitful."

"Long life and prosperity." Navohn lifted his.

Khiann waited for Annani to take hers. "To my love!" He clinked her goblet.

"To my love," she echoed.

He had been expecting more questions, but apparently, the engagement was a done deal. It seemed Ahn was satisfied with Annani's proclamation that she had made up her mind and had no further questions for Khiann.

"Now, tell me, my friend. Where did you find not one, but seven Odus?"

As his father recounted the tale of the Odus finding and following him, and not the other way around, Khiann and Annani smiled at each other like a couple of fools.

It was actually happening.

The impossible was becoming a reality, and it was all thanks to Annani. He would be forever grateful to her for taking the initiative. If not for her, they would not be sitting in the royal reception room discussing the Odus.

"I knew right away that they would be the perfect

wedding gift for Annani," Navohn finished his tale. "It is well known that you are opposed to slavery, my lady." His father turned to Annani. "This is the perfect solution. The seven Odus will serve you and protect you always."

Annani's eyes peeled wide. "I do not understand." While exchanging smiles and coy glances with Khiann, she had not been listening to their fathers' conversation.

"The Odus are not men, Annani," Ahn explained. "They are machines cleverly disguised as people, and these seven are probably the only ones still to exist. They are priceless."

"Oh, wow." Annani glanced at her present. "What am I supposed to do with them?"

Donkey dung. She did not like her gift.

"Whatever you wish. I am sure you will find something. They do not need sleep and can eat garbage. They can also morph their features. So if you prefer female servants, they can become that."

"Everywhere?" A blush spread across her pale cheeks.

Ahn chuckled. "They do not have reproductive organs. What I meant was that they can change their body shape and facial features."

"Oh."

Ahn patted her knee. "What I like most about this amazing gift, though, is that Mortdh could not match it or outdo it."

"My thoughts exactly," Navohn said.

Nai put her goblet down. "It is time to inform Mortdh, is it not?"

"Yes, it is. He must have heard rumors, or what is

more likely was informed by his spies. I was told that a caravan is heading here, loaded with presents for Annani. Mortdh is not aboard. He sent it with his son, Navuh."

"Too little, too late," Annani chimed.

"That is why I am so glad you found the Odus, Navohn. There is nothing in that caravan that can come close to the value of these seven."

Annani shook her head. "I am just glad he is not coming with the caravan. I do not wish to see him."

Ahn picked up his goblet and emptied it in one gulp. "When he gets my message about your upcoming engagement, he will come, and you will have to face him. There is no avoiding that."

8

GULAN

With Annani and her parents conferring with Khiann and his, Gulan had a free evening to do as she pleased. First, though, she had to fold and put away all the dresses Annani had tried on before going to her meeting.

The question was what to do when she was done.

Gulan did not get time off often. Annani hated the substitute maid, complaining about her so much that Gulan had decided it was better not to take her allotted day off and just stay on.

It was not as if she had anything interesting to do with her free day. Most times she had spent it helping her mother with the laundry and Tula with her late homework assignments. It was more work, just of the unpaid kind. At least her lady paid her lavishly for staying the extra day a week.

"Gulan, you have a visitor," Gumer called out from behind the closed door and then opened it. "Esag is waiting for you in your usual place."

"Thank you. I will be out in a moment."

Everyone knew she was training with Khiann's squire. What they did not know was that he had kissed her.

No one knew, not even Annani. Gulan had not told her, mostly because she did not know what to make of it.

Remembering the kiss, she touched a finger to her lips. It had been wonderful, awakening needs and desires she had buried so deep inside that she had not been aware of their existence. Gulan wanted Esag, but what did he want?

Did he want to seduce her?

Did he have feelings for her?

What was his game?

Trying to guess his intentions was driving her crazy. At night, Gulan lay awake, staring at the ceiling for hours while going over every word and every touch. The problem was that she had nothing to base her speculations on.

What did she know about relationships?

Nothing.

Maybe Esag was as tormented as she was and wanted to talk? Perhaps that was why he came? They had not scheduled a training session for this evening. Did he want another kiss?

Did she?

It was about time they had a talk.

Should she change her tunic to a fresh one?

Gazing at the mirror, Gulan tucked a few stray hairs into her braid, tugged on her tunic, and sighed. All her clothes were functional, not pretty. She owned one nice dress, which she wore only to celebrations, and it was not appropriate for a casual meeting in the palace gardens. Especially if all Esag wanted was to show her some new fighting moves.

If he liked her, it was not because of her clothes. Gulan was not like Annani, fretting about outfits and what made her look her best. She was not a princess, only a simple maid.

Flipping her braid back, she lifted her chin and headed out.

In their clearing, she found Esag sitting on the ground with his legs crossed.

"Hi, Gulan. Care to join me?" He patted the dirt next to him.

As she sat on the ground, Gulan was glad to be wearing her simple tunic. "We did not have a session scheduled for this evening, did we?"

"No, but I figured it was a good opportunity to talk to you in private."

As if all the other times they had met in the clearing had not been private. No one paid attention to a squire and a maid practicing fighting moves.

"About what?"

For once, Esag did not look as sure of himself as he usually did. Instead of a smirk, he wore a shy smile, and instead of looking her straight in the eyes, he fidgeted with a twig he had picked up.

"I like you, Gulan, a lot."

Her heart did a happy flip. "I like you too."

He lifted his eyes to her. "A lot?"

She nodded.

"I liked kissing you the other day, and I think you liked it too."

Her ears heating up, she nodded. "It was nice."

Esag snorted. "Nice is not the term I would have used."

"What is wrong with nice?"

"It implies a mediocre kiss. I prefer hot, arousing, earth moving."

It had been all of that and more, but she was too shy to admit it. "If you say so."

"I would like more kisses like that."

So would she.

"I would like much more than kisses."

Gulan blushed and looked away. She wanted that too.

"But I am promised to another, and Khiann is on my case about leading you on."

Her heart did a flip and then sank all the way down to her gut. Her first instinct was to get up and run away like she had done before, but that was the coward's way out, and Gulan was not a coward. She would say what she had to say and then run. "Annani told me. But promises of that kind can be broken. It is not easy, I know, but if you really want to..." She lost her nerve and did not finish her sentence.

"I want to, but I cannot. I do not even like my intended, and the thought of spending the rest of my immortal life with her gives me nightmares, but this joining is crucial to my family. I cannot break the engagement."

Gulan knew all about familial obligations, but that did not make her feel any better. She felt like dying. Esag was not going to break his promise for her. "What is the point of you telling me this? Is it because Khiann ordered you to do so?"

"In part. I want to be honest with you, and I do not want to lead you on. The thing is, I really like being with you. I can imagine us having a life together. A good life."

Esag was twisting the knife deeper and deeper. Why was he so cruel?

"That is neither here nor there. If you cannot break the promise, then you cannot be with me."

Esag broke the twig and tossed it away. "We can be together if you agree to be my concubine. I promise to treat you as if you were my official mate, just without the title. That way I can have the woman I want without destroying my family."

Gulan had stopped listening after the word concubine had left Esag's mouth.

A concubine? That was what he was offering her?

It was such a grave insult that it had left her speechless. Only widows and daughters of destitute families who needed a benefactor accepted such an arrangement. It was just a step above being a whore.

He could have said a lover—it did not imply financial support in exchange for intimate favors, but a concubine?

Not that she would have agreed to that either, but at least she would not have felt so humiliated.

Gulan bolted up. "Do not ever talk to me again."

He caught her hand. "Listen to me, Gulan. It is not as bad as it sounds..."

She yanked her hand out of his grasp. "Yes, it is. Goodbye, Esag. And good luck with the rest of your life."

9

KHIANN

"I am so happy," Annani said as they lay in each other's arms later that night. "Tomorrow, I am going to start planning our engagement party. I am thinking about a procession. We can ride in an open carriage and wave to the crowds while they throw flowers and soft candy at us."

Khiann kissed her forehead. "Is it not a bit much for an engagement party? What will we do for our wedding?"

Annani smiled and stretched her arms. "We can fly in my airboat and throw flowers and candy at the crowd."

"That is a silly idea. If we throw candy from such a great height, it might hurt someone, and flowers will just float away."

"You are right, no flying. Maybe I should save the procession for the wedding?"

"Good choice."

"Do you have anything you would like to add to the celebrations?"

"Nope, I have all I need right here." He closed his arms around her and took her mouth in a hard kiss.

They had made love twice already, but it did not preclude a third time. Now that their secret was officially out, there was no more need for hiding. If they so wished, Khiann could spend every night in Annani's room, and he was definitely going to. Being apart from her during his workday was hard enough. He wanted to spend every moment of his free time with his love.

That was the upside of having their engagement officially announced. The downside was fear of Mortdh.

The moment the news reached Annani's rejected intended, Khiann's life would be in jeopardy. Mortdh would not hesitate to arrange for his assassination. In fact, it was such a likely possibility that Navohn had decided to assign a cadre of bodyguards to go everywhere Khiann went.

Ahn had agreed that it was necessary and even offered the use of his own palace guard.

"Why are you frowning, my love?" Annani smoothed her finger over the ridges that had formed between his eyebrows.

"The usual reason. Mortdh. From now on I cannot go anywhere without an armed escort."

She waved a nonchalant hand. "I think you and our fathers are overreacting. Mortdh will huff and puff, but eventually he will back off. My father is offering him Areana, my half-sister. She is very beautiful and not as argumentative and headstrong as I am. She is a much better choice for Mortdh."

Poor woman. But rather her than Annani.

Khiann lifted a strand of Annani's long hair and wound it around his finger. "She is also a widow, and second in line to the throne, not the first. If anything, Mortdh will feel slighted."

"Then he is a fool. Areana is lovely."

"Not half as lovely as you, my beautiful flower."

As Khiann cupped Annani's small breast, her nipple immediately puckered in his palm. "I prefer to make love again than talk about unpleasant subjects." He leaned and took the hard peak in his mouth.

Nights were for pleasure, their worries and troubles could wait for the light of day.

Annani grinned. "I concur."

10

ANNANI

Something was bothering Gulan.

While Annani was bursting with happiness, her maid had not smiled even once all morning. The girl was not much of a talker, but today she was practically mute. Her lips compressed into a tight line, Gulan seemed to be on the verge of tears.

Did it have anything to do with the upcoming engagement?

Was she worried about her place in Annani's life?

It was true that Khiann was taking up more and more of her time, but that was the natural progression of things. People matured, and their partners took a central place in their lives, especially when the partner was a fated truelove mate.

Nevertheless, even though Khiann had taken Gulan's place as Annani's best friend, the position of second best friend would always and forever belong to Gulan. In fact, Annani had no plans to replace her with another after the joining ceremony. Nai would no doubt want to hire some snooty head maid to run her new household, but Annani wanted Gulan in that position.

Which reminded her that she needed to talk with her mother about her and Khiann's living arrangements. Her father would most likely want her to live in the palace, which meant that a new wing needed to be added to the existing structure.

The other option was for Ekin to move out of the palace and into his own house, and for Annani and Khiann to take over his quarters. But unless Ekin volunteered, no one was going to suggest it. Doing so would be rude.

Perhaps she should go visit him and start dropping hints?

"Gulan, I want to go see my uncle. Do you want to come, or do you want to stay here and tidy up?"

"I will stay."

Damnation. It was not like Gulan. Her maid always wanted to accompany her. Something was bothering the girl, and Annani needed to take care of her friend before worrying about her future accommodations.

"What is wrong, Gulan? Are you afraid of losing my friendship once Khiann and I are joined? Because I can promise you that this will never happen. Wherever I go, you go."

Gulan shook her head. "I do not worry about that, my lady."

"So what is it? You were moping around all day. I do not like seeing you like that. It saddens me, especially when I think it is my fault."

"It has nothing to do with you, my lady. My apologies for casting a shadow on your happiness. This was not my intention." The girl's chin quivered as she tried to hold back tears.

"Come here." Annani opened her arms.

Reluctantly, Gulan accepted the embrace, standing stiff as a broom. The only times she acted like that was when her control was slipping and she was afraid of showing too much emotion.

Silly girl. That was what friends were for. Crying on each other's shoulders was okay.

"Come sit with me and tell me what troubles you." Annani led the girl to the sitting area of her room.

"Talk to me," she commanded.

"It is Esag."

"What did the scoundrel do?"

"He broke my heart." No longer able to contain her pain, Gulan burst into tears, with terrible sobs shaking her big body.

A broken heart could have been a result of many misdeeds. Annani needed to know what exactly Esag had done, in order to mete out a punishment appropriate for his crime. No one hurt her friend and got away with it.

"Tell me what he did."

Gulan wiped her eyes with her sleeve. "He kissed me."

"Against your will?"

"No, I allowed it." She wiped her eyes again. "I had never been kissed before."

"So you were curious. I can understand that. Did he take other liberties you were not comfortable with?"

Esag might have mistakenly assumed that permission for a kiss meant permission for other things as well.

Gulan shook her head. "It was just one kiss. But it was amazing. It made me feel things I did not know I was capable of."

Camel droppings. The poor girl had fallen for the irresponsible squire. "Oh, Gulan, I told you he was unavailable. Did you fall for him? Is that why you are crying?"

She nodded. "But that is not the worst part."

"What could be worse than that if Esag did not overstep his bounds?"

"He asked me to be his concubine."

That did not sound so terrible. In fact, it could have been a good solution to an otherwise insoluble situation.

"And?"

Gulan turned a pair of teary eyes on her. "Is that not enough? It was insulting. I was humiliated. I do not want to ever see him or talk to him again!"

Annani took Gulan's hands. "I am sure that was not his intention. Think of it from his point of view. That is the only way he could be with you without devastating his family. Even if he loves you madly, he cannot break his promise because of his obligation to them. What would you have done in his place?"

Gulan crossed her arms over her ample chest. "I would not have offered him a position as a paid sex servant."

"Is that what you think a concubine is?"

"I was being polite out of respect for you, my lady. A concubine is just one step above a prostitute."

Annani stifled a smile. Angry Gulan was much less

timid and more outspoken than mellow Gulan.

"My half-sister Areana is the daughter of a concubine. Her mother also happens to be a goddess who has a nice cushy temple and worshipers to provide for her. Do you think of her as just a step above a prostitute as well?"

Gulan shrugged. "That is different. She was a concubine to the head god while he was unmated. She was not a toy he kept on the side for when he was bored with his official mate."

So that was the real problem.

Gulan did not want to share Esag. Not that Annani could blame her. If Khiann came to her with such an offer, she would have probably slapped him across the face and sent him away.

Annani could not conceive of sharing the man she loved with another, even if he loved her and not the other female.

Wrapping her arm around Gulan's broad shoulders, Annani sighed. "I understand. It is not about the offer of becoming his concubine. It is about sharing him with another."

Gulan nodded.

"What are you going to do?"

"I do not know, my lady. I will probably cry and cry until there are no more tears left in me. I do not know what else to do."

"Is there anything I can do to help?"

Gulan nodded. "Please do not tell Master Khiann. And if it is possible, try to make it so I do not need to see Esag or talk to him ever again." She put a hand over her breast. "It will hurt too much."

11

MORTDH

The fucking lying son of a whore and his whoring daughter!

Mortdh closed the tablet and tossed it onto his desk, its great value the only reason he had not flung the device against the wall.

It was the only one he owned. To get a replacement, he would have to steal it from another god. There were none to be bought.

Better yet, he could pry one out of his uncle's dead fingers.

Ahn's audacity was boundless. Breaking his promise to Mortdh was bad enough. Delivering the news via tablet was grossly disrespectful.

The little slut had invoked her right of consent. She had chosen to give it to another suitor and by doing so had broken her father's promise to Mortdh.

To try and salvage the situation, he would have no choice but to fly over there and catch up to the caravan.

To impress the slut and Ahn's subjects, Mortdh would enter the city with all the pomp and fanfare of a king.

Escorted by the elite warriors he had sent ahead with Navuh, Mortdh would issue a threat, while offering the wagons filled with gifts as a bribe.

In the meantime, however, with both him and Navuh gone, his stronghold would be left with no proper leadership. The visit would have to be very short.

What a clusterfuck, and it was partially his fault.

Over the years, since the promise had been made, he should have paid his intended more attention. He should have sent her birthday gifts and other nonsense like that. He could have even hired a poet to scribble love poems for her.

Females were stupid and easily manipulated by crap like that. Mortdh just did not expect some young upstart to beat him to it.

If he had wooed her, Annani would not have been as easily swayed by another.

The cunning bastard had stolen her from under Mortdh's nose.

The stupid cunt. She could have joined with the second most powerful god after her father. Instead, she had chosen some young and insignificant god.

Soon to be a dead god.

If Mortdh could not persuade her to change her mind, and she went through with the joining, he was going to make her a widow before she had a chance to conceive.

If she was not pregnant already.

If she were, there were ways to get rid of it.

One way or another, Annani would be his and so would any child she birthed.

Mortdh had begotten many children. Most were worthless humans, but he had several immortal sons who he had been grooming into leadership positions in his army.

However, only Annani could give him a pureblood offspring.

Even if in order to do so he was willing to lower his standards and take an old goddess who had already spread her legs for countless males, it would be impossible to lure one away from her temple and the cushy life she enjoyed.

His only other option was to wait for the next goddess to be born and come of age. The thing was, unless Nai conceived again, she would not be the princess he had been promised.

12

ANNANI

"I do not wish to see him, and there is nothing you can say that will convince me otherwise!" For the first time she could remember, Annani raised her voice in her father's presence.

Mortdh had sent a rider with a message, demanding an audience with Annani and Ahn as soon as he arrived. He was an hour away from the city gates.

"Annani!" her mother gasped.

Ahn only lifted a brow. "Your behavior is that of a child. It is most unbecoming of a soon to be mated woman, not to mention a princess. Did I raise a coward? Are you afraid to face him?"

Annani waved a dismissive hand. "It is pointless. He is going to try and change my mind, and when that does not happen, he will start issuing threats. Then you will offer him Areana, there will be some back and forth negotiations, and he will go home either satisfied or not. Instead, you can skip right to the negotiation part and spare me the unpleasantness." Annani crossed her arms over her chest. "And anyway, how did he get here so fast? You told me he was not on the caravan heading this way."

"He flew in."

Annani plopped down on the divan and rubbed her temples. "How long does it take a caravan to get here from his stronghold?"

"Two to three weeks," her father said. "His spies must have informed him about Khiann's tutoring. Mortdh is not stupid and must have suspected something. He decided to send you gifts as a preemptive measure."

As if he could woo her with material things. Only a pompous ass like Mortdh would presume to know what she wanted without bothering to get to know her. "And after getting your message, he decided to come here and try to change my mind."

Ahn nodded. "Precisely."

"Ugh. What do you want me to do, Father? I do not know what to say to him without making him even angrier."

"First of all, you need to watch your temper and act like a mature and levelheaded woman. Do not let Mortdh rile you. Be polite but firm, and emphasize why you are bound by tradition to choose Khiann over him. The Fates sent you your one true love, and you cannot anger them by refusing to accept their bounty."

"That actually sounds good."

"I know. I spent a lot of time thinking how to phrase it in the least offensive way I could. This is what I wrote in my message to him and what you should keep saying. You are not to blame. It is the Fates' will."

Annani shook her head. "And yet, he flew here right after reading it, which means that he does not believe in the Fates."

"Of course he does not believe in them. But Mortdh is vain, and his biggest issue is the insult of a broken promise. Blaming the Fates will help him save face in the public's eyes."

Nai rose to her feet and joined Annani on the divan. "Courage, my child, I know it is difficult, and that you would rather have done anything but deal with Mortdh. But think of it this way. After this unpleasantness is over with, there will be nothing but joy. Right?" She hooked a finger under Annani's chin. "You have been so brave in your pursuit of happiness. Do not falter at the very end, when you can practically touch the finish line with your fingertips."

Taking a deep breath, Annani squeezed her mother's hand. "You always know the right thing to say. I can do this."

Nai patted her knee. "That is my girl. The future ruler of the realm."

Funny, at that moment Annani did not feel like the ruler of anything. Nevertheless, her mother was right. It was the last hurdle on the road. Once Mortdh was dealt with, it was going to be smooth riding the rest of the way.

Provided he did not leave enraged.

Which meant that she had to summon all of her meager diplomatic abilities and keep smiling even when she felt like tearing Mortdh's head off his body, which given his attitude was bound to happen.

Ugh, she should have paid better attention to the

court proceedings her father had forced her to attend. As it was, the only thing that came to mind was to channel her mother's regal demeanor and keep her mouth shut as much as possible.

"I will take my leave now to get ready. Could you send for me when he gets here?"

Her father nodded.

Ahn looked somber, more than usual. Was he worried?

He was always so sure of himself. She had never seen him with anything other than a confident and regal expression on his face. As the ruler of gods, immortals, and humans, there was no one higher than Ahn. He had no one to answer to other than the big assembly, and he had the power of veto over them too.

If he was worried, he must have had a good reason.

As Annani walked back to her room, the mute Gulan trailing behind her, she wondered what else she could do to help her father. Maybe she should force herself to be really nice to Mortdh and pay him a lot of compliments?

Her father had said Mortdh was vain. Vain people liked to hear how great they were. The problem was that she could think of nothing good to say about him.

Maybe he was good-looking and she could comment on that. And she should thank him profusely for the gifts he brought her. Perhaps she should refuse them? After all, she was not going to accept him, so it was not fair to keep the gifts.

On the other hand, he might take offense at that.

Dear Fates, what should I do?

13

AHN

As Ahn sat on his throne with his mate on one side and his daughter on the other, he was keenly aware of Areana's presence behind the privacy partition. Even the heavy perfume of incense could not mask the scent of her anxiety from his superior sense of smell.

It was good that Mortdh's nose was not as discriminating. More predatory in nature than most gods, Mortdh might react aggressively to the scent of her fear and become even more combative than usual.

It was the exact opposite of what Ahn wished to achieve.

After many hours of pondering the problem, he had arrived at a solution that might be acceptable to both of them. At the very least, it should avert war for several thousands of years.

Or so he hoped.

It had been a strategic decision to hide Areana until the

moment he presented her to Mortdh. Dressed in the finest of gowns, her hair artfully done by Nai's personal hairdresser, she looked resplendent. Hopefully, Mortdh would be dazzled enough by the gentle beauty to overlook her being a widow and not the fresh young thing he desired.

Unlike her half-sister's, Annani's scent revealed no anxiety, only determination. Despite her impetuous nature, she would make a fine ruler one day. Annani had guts and a good head on her shoulders. All she needed were a few hundreds of years to mature.

"Let the games begin," he murmured as servants opened the double doors to the throne room.

Mortdh sauntered in as if he owned the place, his chest puffed up, and his head held high. A few paces behind him, his son Navuh sported the exact same expression.

Had they rehearsed it before coming in?

Ahn rose to his feet and descended the three steps that separated the dais from the rest of the throne room. Extending his arms, he offered Mortdh a broad smile. "Welcome, nephew. It is so good of you to visit."

To his credit, Mortdh followed protocol, returning the embrace and the mutual back-clapping. "Thank you, uncle, for welcoming my son and me into your home." He motioned for Navuh to come closer.

Offering a perfunctory bow, Navuh submitted to the same greeting.

So far so good.

As the two sat in the chairs facing the dais, Ahn returned to his throne, drew back his robe, and sat down.

"May I proceed directly to the reason for my visit?" Mortdh asked.

Ahn nodded. "Please, speak freely, nephew. We are a family. We can dispense with unnecessary chitchat." He could have dragged it out longer by insisting on small talk and requesting updates, which would most likely have been all fake, but while Ahn would have enjoyed the game tremendously, Annani and Areana would not.

For their sakes, he was going to make this circus show as short and to the point as possible while still achieving his goals.

Not sparing Annani a glance, Mortdh addressed Ahn. "I understand that the princess believes she has found her fated truelove, but I beg to differ. Annani is still very young and impressionable. She has fallen into the clutches of a usurper."

Next to Ahn, Annani bristled, but she kept her mouth shut.

Smart girl.

"Do you not trust me to ensure the virtue of a contender for my daughter's hand?"

Mortdh smiled evilly, his thoughts transparent. After all, Ahn had promised his daughter to him—a god as far from virtuous as it got. But this was not about truth, this was about saving face and playing a game—one that both he and Ahn knew how to play well.

Mortdh bowed his head in mock respect. "Naturally, my lord. But you are too busy with affairs of state to pay close attention to your daughter."

Before Ahn had a chance to respond, Mortdh lifted his hand in the sign for peace. "I am guilty of the same. I should have paid better attention to my precious intended. In my defense, I have waited for her to reach the age of majority before coming to court her as a young woman, and not a child. But just as you, my lord, I have been preoccupied with affairs of state and waited too long. I am here to rectify my negligence."

Mortdh turned to Navuh. "Please have my lovely intended's gifts brought in."

"Of course, Father." Navuh pushed to his feet and bowed to Mortdh, bending his head much lower than he had done for Ahn.

It did not escape Ahn's notice that Mortdh was still referring to Annani as his intended.

As the guards opened the doors for Navuh, he signaled for those waiting outside to enter. A well-organized procession began, with servants bringing in large baskets filled with beautiful fabrics and colorful scarfs, and smaller ones overflowing with gold and silver jewelry.

The procession ended with a large group of unusually pale humans. Upon entering, they immediately dropped to the floor in a deep obeisance.

"Who are these people?" Annani asked, speaking for the first time.

Ahn had never seen the likes of them either. Unlike the humans he was familiar with, who were olive skinned or darker and had black hair, these humans had lost most of their pigmentation. They must have been northern dwellers where the sun was very weak, forcing them to adapt.

Ahn was familiar with the phenomenon.

The gods' home world was almost completely

devoid of light, which resulted in them developing luminous skin and glowing eyes.

"Exotic slaves captured in the north," Mortdh said with pride in his voice.

Annani let out a most unladylike growl. "Slaves? You brought me slaves as gifts?"

Ahn shushed her with a quick wave of his hand. "Did all these people sell themselves into slavery, Mortdh?"

Slavery was strictly regulated and allowed only in very specific circumstances. Capturing free people and enslaving them was not one of them.

"No, but these are savages, my lord. They hardly qualify as people. They are nomads who hunt for their sustenance. It is like capturing a herd of wild horses. You would not ask a horse if it wants to serve, would you?"

14

ANNANI

If Annani hated Mortdh before, she utterly despised him now. What a condescending and heartless buffoon.

"I would not say that primitive people who lack culture are equivalent to horses. But I will let it slide this time. In the future, though, you should adhere to the law, nephew. After all, without laws we are no better than these savages, am I right?"

Good for you, Father.

Once the idiot left, she was going to free these poor people. The question was what should she do with them?

Despite their almost god-like paleness, they looked indeed savage. Long tangled hair that had not ever seen a comb, and clothes made from hides and fur, which probably made them swelter in the southern heat.

Poor creatures. Could they even talk?

Mortdh inclined his head. "I thought the princess

would be awed by creatures never seen before in these parts."

Annani did not answer even though Mortdh was looking directly at her. If she did, nothing nice was going to come out of her mouth.

Her father answered for her. "I am sure she is. Annani is very inquisitive. She would love to learn about the northern lands from these people. Please have them escorted out. My servants will provide them with a meal."

That was actually true. She was very curious to hear all about distant lands and what kinds of plant and animal life they supported, provided she could converse with them. They probably spoke a foreign language she would have to learn.

As Mortdh signaled Navuh to take the bunch of poor savages out of the throne room, the palace servants took the opportunity to collect the baskets of goods and line them up against the wall.

Annani regarded the offerings with thinly veiled disgust. Apparently, Mortdh thought of her as a commodity he could trade for. She was not a peasant's daughter to be gifted a couple of sheep. Much thought was usually given to a proper engagement gift for a highborn lady, not just piles of randomly accumulated stuff.

"My dear nephew," Ahn said as the throne room emptied of servants. "I appreciate the effort you put into trying to convince Annani to accept you, but I am afraid the Fates have made up their minds and chosen another for her. I for one do not want to tangle with them lest they retaliate, and neither should you."

Mortdh made a move to stand, but Ahn lifted a hand. "Hear me out, nephew. I think I have a solution that would be satisfactory to all parties involved. From the start, this joining was about politics and not love, a way for us to solidify our ties. We can still have that. I can no longer give you my daughter Annani, but I can give you my other daughter, Areana."

Ahn got up, walked toward the partition, and offered his hand to his older daughter. "I present the lovely Areana."

As Ahn led her down the stairs to where Mortdh was sitting in front of the dais, the poor woman trembled all over.

His eyes glowing with fury at Ahn, Mortdh barely spared her a glance.

Navuh, on the other hand, stifled a gasp when she lifted her head and looked at his father. Had he been infatuated with Areana? Surely this was not the first time he was seeing her.

She was indeed very beautiful, but Mortdh was too busy fuming to notice.

"A widow," Mortdh hissed. "Used goods."

While Areana blushed and lowered her head, Annani felt like taking off her sandals and chucking them at the brute.

What a nasty thing to say.

Ahn ignored the rude comment. "Areana is my daughter and second in line to the throne. What is more, she agrees to the joining. It can be done today if you so wish."

Mortdh finally deigned to spare her a glance. "She is pleasing to the eye, I will admit that. But you need to sweeten the deal. I am getting the short end of the stick here, and I do not like it. You promised me Annani, the first in line to the throne, not the second, and at the time an untouched virgin, not a used woman."

As Ahn led the trembling Areana up the dais and helped her to a seat, Annani wanted to rush to her sister and hug her, offer her some comfort, but she could not. The negotiations were about to start, and she needed to sit quietly and let her father do what he did best.

"I had a feeling that would be your sentiment, nephew, and I came up with a plan that should be most satisfactory to you. Come, join me at the table."

Ahn stepped down and walked over to where a table stood against the wall. Annani had wondered about what it was doing there, as it was not part of the throne room's regular decor. She had suspected that the large scroll resting upon it was a map.

As Mortdh followed her father, Ahn unfurled the scroll and spread it over the table. "Here is my territory." Ahn pointed to the large area nestled between the two rivers. "And here is yours." He pointed to Mortdh's stronghold, situated on top of a mountain overlooking the middle sea.

"As it is," Ahn continued. "There is hardly any contact between the two regions. I am offering you sovereignty over yours. Not complete, you will still need to abide by our laws, but you can be a king of your own territory. Instead of you being subject to my rule, we will form a sort of federation. If any of the gods decide to join you, they will be subject to your rule."

Mortdh rubbed his hand over his short beard. "An

interesting proposition, but how does it differ from what is already the situation?"

"It makes it legal. You seek acknowledgment and royal succession, correct? Now you have it. My line will continue through Annani and her offspring, and yours will continue through Areana and hers." Ahn threaded the fingers of his hands. "Two intertwined monarchies. Instead of having to wait thousands of years for me to step down, you can be king tomorrow. With my congratulations."

Wow, and wow.

Her father's idea was not only revolutionary but potentially dangerous. Splitting the gods and creating two centers of power could lead to conflicts of interest and eventually war. But that was a worry for the distant future.

Ahn was taking care of the current crisis.

Mortdh was getting almost everything he wanted without giving anything up. Except for her, but he was not really interested in Annani as a person. She had been just a means to an end, which her father was handing to him on a golden platter.

"Is my proposition satisfactory to you, nephew?"

Mortdh was still staring at the map as he nodded. "I am claiming this entire region." He made a big circle with his finger.

"Deal." Her father offered his hand.

When Mortdh shook it, Annani let out a breath.

It was over.

The last hurdle had been surmounted.

Nothing else was standing in her path to eternal happiness with her beloved.

15

MORTDH

"That went well," Navuh said as they returned to the caravan parked outside the city limits. "Ahn's offer was very generous. It is almost everything you wanted, Father."

"Not even close." Mortdh slammed his fist into the side of a wagon. "I agreed to his proposal to throw him off. We keep on building our army and getting ready to take over by force. I do not want to be king of the Northern Territory. I want what I have always wanted and what should have been my birthright. I want to rule over them all. Gods, immortals, and humans."

"So what now?" Navuh asked.

Mortdh continued walking in the direction of his flyer. "I left one of your less competent brothers in charge while I was gone. I need to get back. You will bring the caravan home."

"What about Areana?"

Mortdh waved a dismissive hand. "Bring her with you. I promised Ahn a joining ceremony in two moon cycles, but I do not think I will actually go through with it. Fuck Ahn. After the way he humiliated me, I am planning on humiliating him by keeping his daughter as a concubine instead of an official mate."

Navuh rubbed his hand over his jaw. "But she is a goddess. You always wanted a pureblooded child."

Mortdh clapped his son's back. "You are only an immortal, but I could not have asked for a more capable and enterprising son. You are my successor."

"Thank you, Father." Navuh bowed deeply and kissed the back of his hand.

Navuh was indeed a good son, but if Mortdh had a child with Annani, a male child, he would become Mortdh's successor. For now, though, Navuh did not need to know it.

Areana did not merit the same status. Being Ahn's daughter was irrelevant because she was second in line.

Then again, if he arranged for Annani's untimely demise, Areana would become first in line, and he could resume his original plan. The thing was, it would not be easy to assassinate the princess, and even if he succeeded, the other gods would never forgive him for taking out their darling and would turn against him.

Then there was the issue of Ahn. The fucker was in no hurry to step down, and his assassination would be even harder to pull off than that of his precious daughter.

Mortdh took in a long calming breath. He was in no rush. Nothing needed to be decided right away. He was going to take his time and plot the most beneficial course of action.

For him.

Taking another deep breath, Mortdh tried to extinguish the inferno of anger burning inside him but failed. Thoughts of someone else screwing Annani kept the fire going. The only thing that could restore his calm was taking the fucker out.

He could get rid of the usurper, and then take Annani with her consent or without.

Not yet, though. Mortdh needed to think everything through.

For the time being, though, until he decided his next move, the position of his official mate should remain open.

He should definitely not join with Areana.

16

KHIANN

As Khiann sat in the open carriage and waved at the cheering crowds, he felt quite ridiculous, sitting there in the finest of garments and smiling like a fool at the humans and immortals gathered on the streets. That being said, he had to concede that Annani's idea to have a procession, or rather three of them, was an excellent crowd-pleaser, generating an enormous amount of goodwill toward the royal family.

Instead of the two of them riding in the carriage after the ceremony, she had flipped the order, having them arriving in separate ones, each followed by dozens of entertainers, most of whom were guards in disguise.

Khiann and Annani were not fooling themselves that all was well and they were safe. Mortdh had seemed appeased by Ahn's generous offer, but he was unpredictable. Even Ekin, Mortdh's own father, had warned them against getting complacent and slacking on security.

Some of the entertainers, however, were the real

deal, dancers and singers. For the occasion, a song had been composed by a famous poet, celebrating love's triumph and telling the tale of Annani falling in love and choosing a commoner over the powerful Mortdh.

Not that Khiann considered himself a commoner, but the crowds were eating it up. If Mortdh tried to contest the joining, he would find no support from the people.

Even Ahn was impressed with his daughter's ability to manipulate public opinion. He had said she was better at it than he, and that it would have never crossed his mind to bother with influencing the masses.

Annani had an innate talent for creating just the right amount of fanfare and drama to endear her to everyone, including gods, immortals, and humans.

As had been planned, the two processions arrived at the palace gates at the same time and were supposed to enter its inner walls side by side.

On the spur of the moment though, Kian leaped from his carriage into Annani's and took her into his arms.

The crowd went wild, cheering and hooting long after the two carriages had passed the gates, leaving the entertainers behind to lead the festivities outside.

"That was amazing!" Annani beamed as the gates closed behind them. "Much better than I expected. They love us, Khiann." She wrapped her arms around his neck and kissed him in front of all the invited guests, who included gods, prominent immortals, and even several human dignitaries.

"They love you, my beautiful flower. I am just an accessory." Khiann jumped out of the carriage and lifted his arms to help Annani down, clasping her to his chest instead of letting her sandaled feet touch the ground.

Her elaborate gown and headdress were beautiful but looked heavy and uncomfortable to walk in.

She slapped his arm and whispered, "Let me down, Khiann. We are supposed to walk in hand in hand, not with you carrying me inside."

He lifted a brow. "Who said there is only one way to do it? Look around you, love."

People were smiling at them.

One of the goddesses wiped happy tears from her eyes, while another started clapping, soon to be followed by the rest of their guests.

With a triumphant grin, he dipped his head and kissed her softly, then whispered in her ear, "They like the spontaneity. It shows our love for each other better than anything rehearsed."

Annani relaxed in his arms and whispered back, "It seems I am not the only one with a knack for crowd-pleasing. You are a natural."

He smiled. "I learn from the best."

Holding his princess in his arms, Khiann ran up the steps to the palace's front doors, but he had to slow down as he entered the gallery leading into the grand hall where their parents were waiting for them. Its walls were lined with guests who needed to be acknowledged. Smiles greeted them everywhere, with people returning Annani's waves and air kisses.

Everyone loved the spontaneous display. Except for Nai, who frowned as they entered the hall.

Apparently, Annani's mother was a stickler for

protocol and did not approve of Khiann's unorthodox delivery of her daughter.

But she was the only one. Ahn nodded and smiled, while Khiann's parents grinned from ear to ear.

Six throne-like chairs were set upon a dais, and Khiann deposited Annani into one of the middle ones. Her parents took the chairs on his bride's side, while his parents sat in the ones on his.

The next couple of hours or so were spent greeting the guests. Lined up outside in the gallery, they were admitted one at the time, walked in, climbed the steps to the right of the dais, offered their congratulations, and then descended the steps to its left.

When they were done, servants escorted them to their tables.

It was all very formal, orderly, and incredibly boring. Next to him, Annani kept tapping her sandaled feet on the floor until her mother cast her a withering glance and she stopped. But she had not let the smile slip from her face even once while greeting her guests.

When everyone was finally seated, Ahn rose to his feet and lifted his hands to hush the murmuring.

"Dear guests. Thank you for coming to celebrate this joyous occasion with us. Annani and Khiann have been uniquely blessed by the Fates. They are each other's fated trueloves, and as we all know, that which the Fates decree must come to pass."

He paused, letting the crowd show their approval with prolonged applause.

"Today, they will pledge their lives to each other, but this is only a formality. In their hearts, they have done so already weeks ago. That is why it was decided to combine the engagement and joining ceremonies into one."

He waved his hand at Khiann and his daughter. "These two are young and impatient to start their lives together."

Believing the romantic spin, the guests clapped and cheered.

The decision to combine the ceremonies, however, was not due to impatience. It had been Ekin's idea. With Mortdh's unpredictable nature, or insanity as Khiann thought of the god's unstable mental state, it was better to finalize things as soon as possible.

Ahn waited for the applause and cheers to subside before continuing. "As one who has been similarly blessed, I know how incredibly precious this gift is." He turned and offered his hand to his mate, helping her up. "I wish Annani and Khiann a long and happy life filled with as much love and joy as Nai and I share."

As a new round of applause erupted, Nai dipped her head. "Thank you," she said when it subsided, and then sat back.

Her mate remained standing. "Ring bearers, approach!" he called out.

It was custom to choose a best friend to do the honors, but gods usually chose other gods as their ring bearers, not immortal servants. Again veering away from tradition, Annani had chosen Gulan as hers, while Khiann had chosen Esag.

The two had not seen or talked to each other for weeks, but Khiann had no idea what had caused the falling out. Annani knew, but Gulan had asked her to keep it a secret.

Esag, who had been uncharacteristically tightlipped and moody lately, had refused to talk about it too.

Other than Mortdh's looming threat, the spat between those two was the only thing casting dark shadows on this otherwise joyous night.

With a bow, Esag presented Khiann with a silver tray holding Annani's ring, while Gulan presented Annani with Khiann's. Once the rings were in their hands, the two bowed and retreated without sparing each other a single glance.

"And now that we have the rings, it is time for the pledge," Ahn announced. "The young couple have decided to prepare their own instead of me reciting some old and overused lines."

A few guests chuckled before another round of applause started.

As Khiann and Annani pushed to their feet and faced each other, Khiann smiled at his tiny bride. Without her headdress, she barely reached the middle of his chest, but the ornament was so tall that the top of it reached his nose.

Was that why she had chosen it? Did she want to make herself look taller because he towered over her?

Silly girl. As small as she was, all eyes were on her and not on Khiann. Annani's mesmerizing beauty and inner power shone so brightly that no one could avert their eyes even for a second to spare him a glance.

It was as it should be.

Annani was the heart of their people, the beacon of light for their future, while he was there to keep her happy and shining bright. He was the pedestal upon which she could stand and the pillar against which she could lean.

Nothing more.

And yet he counted himself the luckiest male alive.

"My love, my life, my everything," Annani started her pledge. "Against all the odds, and despite many obstacles, the Fates have brought us together. I will forever be grateful for this most precious of gifts. I do not know what I have done to merit such a boon, to find my one and only and experience this incredible love that is going to sustain me for thousands and thousands of years."

She turned to look at Khiann's parents. "Thank you, Fates, and thank you Yaeni and Navohn for the gift that is your son."

As his mother wiped happy tears from her eyes, Annani turned back to Khiann. "And thank you, Khiann, for taking a risk on me. I promised to make it worth your while, and I am going to keep that promise forever."

As she lifted the ring, he offered her his hand. "Tradition dictates that I say; with this ring, I bind you to me. But a ring is only a symbol of what is in one's heart. So instead, I am going to say; this ring, which is made from an unbreakable alloy, symbolizes the strength of our unbreakable bond." She threaded the band on his finger. "In front of all these witnesses, I, Annani daughter of Nai and Ahn, pronounce you, Khiann son of Yaeni and Navohn, as mine, and I pledge myself to you for eternity and beyond."

His mind reeling, his heart so full it felt like bursting, Khiann forgot all the beautiful words he had prepared.

Taking Annani's hand, he repeated her words to her. "My love, my life, my everything. I promise to spend the rest of my life making you happy and thanking the Fates and your parents for the precious gift of you."

He put the ring on her slender finger. "In front of all these witnesses, I, Khiann son of Yaeni and Navohn, pronounce you, Annani daughter of Nai and Ahn, as mine, and I pledge myself to you for eternity and beyond."

17

ANNANI

"Good morning, my love." Khiann woke Annani with a kiss.

Yawning, she stretched her arms and legs, then hugged the blanket to her chest and rolled to her side. "I want to sleep more."

The joining ceremony had been marvelous, but also exhausting.

Annani might have overdone it with the celebrations, but given that it was a once in a lifetime event, she did not want to skimp on anything.

Claiming security concerns, Khiann and her father had not been too enthusiastic about the post-ceremony carriage ride through the city she had arranged for, but Annani had insisted.

She was so glad she had.

Joy and love needed to be shared and celebrated.

The carriage had been beautifully decorated with flowers and ribbons, and the people had been delighted to see her and Khiann riding in it as a mated couple.

Even though it had been late at night when they had ridden through the streets, it had seemed as if every last human in the city had forgone sleep to go out and cheer them on.

Khiann kissed her neck. "One of your Odus brought us breakfast. I think it was Okidu, but I have a hard time telling them apart."

She had given them each a name, instead of the general term Odu, which referred to what they were, but not who they were as individuals. Supposedly, they were all the same, but their ability to morph their features translated into slight differences that made them look more like brothers than identical twins.

Khiann's father had explained that they lacked personality and she should not read too much into it just because they looked so human, but Annani had a feeling that was not entirely true. Something other than programming must have prompted them to adopt the slight differences.

Their arrival had made Gulan's work much easier. They had taken over all the cleaning and fetching, but Gulan still did Annani's hair and helped her with getting dressed.

"Where is Gulan?" Annani asked.

"I have not seen her since last night."

That was odd.

"Could you send one of the Odus to look for her? I need to get dressed."

"What for? You can eat breakfast naked." He waggled his brows.

She could, after all, the Odus were not really men, and her nudity had no effect on them. Except, she did not feel comfortable enough around them yet. But if her mate wanted a morning romp, she could send them away.

Annani was all for it.

"You can tell the Odus to leave us, and we can have some fun," she husked, pulling the blanket just enough to give Khiann a glimpse of her breast.

He sucked in a breath but shook his head. "Food first, lovemaking second. I feel guilty for further exhausting you last night. I should have let you sleep when we returned."

"Do not be silly. It would have not been a joining night without an actual joining."

He smiled sheepishly. "Yeah, but I kept you awake for hours."

That he had. "Come here." She lifted her arms, inviting him to come back to bed.

Instead, he leaned into the embrace and kissed her. "Food, love, you need nourishment. I will send Okidu or one of the others to find Gulan. Or, if you please, I can serve as your maid and help you get dressed." He winked.

"Then we will not get to eat for sure."

"You are right, my love." He kissed her forehead.

As Khiann stepped out of the bedchamber to talk to the Odus, Annani pulled the blanket up to her nose and closed her eyes. She could catch a few more moments of sleep before he came back.

"Annani, my love, wake up," Khiann said.

Something in his tone jolted her awake in an instant. "What happened?"

He handed her a small scroll tied with a pretty

ribbon. "The Odus searched everywhere. Gulan is not in the palace. They found this in her room. It is from her. It is addressed to you."

"What is in it?"

Despite the knot forming in her gut, Annani hoped the scroll was a gift from Gulan—a wish of happy joining, or maybe a poem—and not bad news.

"I did not open it."

Snatching it from his hand, Annani removed the ribbon and unfurled the scroll. As she had thought, it started with good wishes, but unfortunately, it did not end with them.

"What does it say?" Khiann asked.

"She is gone," Annani whispered as tears pooled in the corners of her eyes. "Gulan ran away because she was broken-hearted and could not stay and watch Esag join with his intended."

"Donkey dung!" Khiann exclaimed. "I told the idiot not to toy with her feelings."

With tears sliding down her cheeks, Annani handed him the scroll. "It is not only about Esag. She says that I do not need her anymore because I have you to love and the Odus to serve me. She begs me to help her family by taking Tula in her place. They need the income."

Khiann read the note, then rose to his feet and started pacing while raking his hands through his hair. "Do you have any idea where she might have gone?"

Annani shook her head. "I do not. But she could not have gone far. She was still here last night to help me undress. Even if she left right away, she could not have traversed a long distance on foot. She does not own a horse."

"I will send Esag after her."

"Do you think it is wise? Even if he finds her, she will refuse to come back with him." It pained Annani to say it, but Gulan was a free woman, and if she wanted to quit her employment, it was her right to do so. "Maybe we should respect her wishes and let her go?"

Khiann stopped his pacing and came back to sit on the bed next to Annani. "You would have been right if she went home or to her next place of employment, but she did not. From her note, I understand that she wants to disappear and go somewhere no one knows her. For starters, it is not safe for a female to travel alone, even a strong one like Gulan, and secondly, where could she go where no one knows her?" He lifted a brow.

That was a good question. As Annani's maid, Gulan was well known. Maybe not by name, but her unusual size ensured that everyone who had ever seen her, remembered her. There was only one settlement of immortals who were unfamiliar with her.

"She could not be so stupid. You think she is heading to Mortdh's territory?"

"Where else?"

"But that is insane!"

Khiann clasped her hand to his chest. "Love can make even the most rational person do crazy things."

"And beautiful things," Annani said. "Love is the force behind most everything we do. Good and bad. Right and wrong."

The end... for now...

Dear reader,

Thank you for reading **GODDESS'S CHOICE.** If you enjoyed the story, I would be grateful if you could leave a **short review** on Amazon. (With a few words, you'll make me very happy. :-))

The Children of the Gods Origins story continues in

GODDESS'S HOPE

AREANA'S STORY

Flip the page to read an excerpt and find out where Gulan is heading.

EXCERPT: GODDESS'S HOPE

GULAN

Annani and Khiann's joining ceremony had been beautiful. The love between them had shone so brightly that even the most cynical of guests had been moved, especially during the exchange of vows.

Several had even shed a few tears.

Gulan had shed a lot, but not for the same reason.

Tonight, after she'd helped Annani out of her ceremonial attire, Gulan was leaving.

She might never see her best friend again.

The smile she had plastered on her face was so fake, it would have never fooled Annani if her mind was not as full of Khiann as it was. Or maybe her lady was just too happy to notice.

Gods, it was so difficult to keep from crying openly when Gulan felt as if she were dying inside. With a tremendous effort, she held on until the preparations for the mating night were finished and she bid Annani goodnight. But as soon as the door to the newly-mated couple's bedchamber closed behind her, the tears burst free, running down her cheeks and wresting pitiful sobs out of her.

Leaving was so hard. But staying was harder.

Thank the gods, Gulan did not encounter anyone as she ran all the way to the servants' quarters. In the privacy of her own room, she leaned against the closed door and cried even harder.

She was being ungrateful.

The private chamber that Gulan did not have to share with another maid was just one more kindness out of the many her lady had bestowed upon her throughout the years. While the rest of the palace staff slept two and three to a room, Gulan had the entire bedchamber to herself.

And how was she repaying it?

By running away and leaving a cowardly note behind.

The decision to leave had been the hardest Gulan had ever made in her life, but an unavoidable one. The pain of losing Esag, or rather the dream of him, was too much for her to bear. If she stayed, she would have to watch him join with another, and Gulan knew she would not survive that.

It was better to start a new life somewhere far away from Esag.

She would go on an adventure and travel to distant lands. Until the pain subsided, Gulan would fill her life with the exploration of the different human cultures Esag had told her about. If traders went there on a regular basis, so could she. People who produced goods and engaged in trade could not be completely uncivilized. The gods' teachings must have reached them.

Wiping away her tears with the sleeve of her beautiful new dress, Gulan took a deep breath and sighed. After weeks of planning, it was finally time.

Maybe in a year or two, once she had healed enough, Gulan would come back and tell Annani about all she had seen.

She needed to get moving, though. The caravan she was joining was heading out at sunrise, which was in a couple of hours.

Pushing away from the door, Gulan walked over to her bed, took off the dress Annani had commissioned for her for the ceremony, folded it carefully, and put it on top of the mattress.

Where Gulan was going, she would have no need for it. In fact, since she was going as a young man, not a woman, she would have no need for any feminine garb.

It was quite ironic that after a lifetime of resenting her height and strength, she was taking advantage of them. The caravan organizer was always looking for capable, strong men who could lift heavy cargo and defend the caravan if needed.

Even Esag's combat training would come in handy.

Standing in front of a mirror with a pair of shears in hand, Gulan took hold of her thick braid and hesitated for only a moment before hacking it off. What was left fanned out around her face, the jagged edges looking as haggard and sad as her soul.

With several quick snips, she evened it out to look like an acceptable hairstyle for a man. Dipping her fingers in a pouch filled with soot, she smeared it over her chin. Hopefully, it would pass as a shadow of a beard.

Her face was still too feminine to belong to a male, but with her size, no one would question her gender. They would assume she was a young man with a girly face.

It happened.

The next step was to bind her breasts and put on the peasant clothes she had bought. Under the tunic, she tied a pouch full of coins. Some of it was what she had managed to save up, but most of it came from selling the necklace Annani had given her. It was enough to keep her fed for a year.

With what she was going to get paid for working in the caravan, Gulan had nothing to worry about—except for Tula, her parents, and Annani.

Leaving behind the people she loved was the hardest part. But they would manage without her—provided Annani would not be too angry at her for running away and would help her family.

Gulan trusted her lady's kind heart would not turn vindictive.

The truth was that Annani no longer needed her. With Khiann to keep her company and the Odus serving her lady's every need, a maid was superfluous. But even if Annani decided to send riders after her, she would not know in which direction Gulan was heading.

No one would expect her to choose the distant Nile valley as her final destination.

GODDESS'S HOPE

Is coming out October 2018

TO READ AN EXTENDED EXCERPT FROM

DARK STRANGER THE DREAM

Book 1 in the

THE CHILDREN OF THE GODS SERIES

JOIN

The Children Of The Gods

***VIP Club* at**

itlucas.com

And get the access code to the VIP Portal

THE CHILDREN OF THE GODS ORIGINS

ANNANI'S STORY

1: GODDESS'S CHOICE

AREANA'S STORY

2: GODDESS'S HOPE

THE CHILDREN OF THE GODS

KIAN & SYSSI'S STORY

1: DARK STRANGER THE DREAM

2: DARK STRANGER REVEALED

3: DARK STRANGER IMMORTAL

DARK STRANGER TRILOGY + GODDESS'S CHOICE—PART 1

AMANDA'S STORY

4: DARK ENEMY TAKEN

5: DARK ENEMY CAPTIVE

6: DARK ENEMY REDEEMED

KRI & MICHAEL'S STORY

6.5: MY DARK AMAZON NOVELLA

ANDREW'S STORY

7: DARK WARRIOR MINE

8: DARK WARRIOR'S PROMISE

9: DARK WARRIOR'S DESTINY

10: DARK WARRIOR'S LEGACY

BHATHIAN & EVA'S STORY

11: DARK GUARDIAN FOUND

12: DARK GUARDIAN CRAVED

13: DARK GUARDIAN'S MATE

Brundar & Calypso's Story

14: Dark Angel's Obsession

15: Dark Angel's Seduction

16: Dark Angel's Surrender

Turner's Story

17: Dark Operative: A Shadow of Death

18: Dark Operative: A Glimmer of Hope

19: Dark Operative: The Dawn of Love

Anandur's Story

20: Dark Survivor Awakened

21: Dark Survivor Echoes of Love

22: Dark Survivor Reunited

Magnus & Vivian's Story

23: Dark Widow's Secret

If you're already a subscriber and forgot the password to the VIP portal, you can find it at the bottom of each of my emails. Or click HERE to retrieve it.

You can also email me at isabell@itlucas.com

FOR A FREE NARRATION OF

GODDESS'S CHOICE

AND A SNEAK PEEK AT GODDESS'S HOPE

JOIN

THE VIP CLUB AT

ITLUCAS.COM

AVAILABLE ONLY ON THE VIP PORTAL AT ITLUCAS.COM

FREE AUDIOBOOK, PREVIEW CHAPTERS, AND OTHER GOODIES OFFERED ONLY TO MY VIPS.

ACKNOWLEDGMENTS

First, I want to thank you for reading and joining me on this incredible adventure.

When I pressed the "Publish" button in July of 2015, I never expected the special connection I'd form with my readers. My circle of friends suddenly expanded exponentially.

I love answering your emails, responding to your Facebook comments and messages, and reading your reviews. You are literally the wind beneath my creative wings, providing the motivation for the endless hours that go into writing, editing, and publishing my stories.

Which brings me to my family. My husband and our four sons are so amazingly supportive and accepting. Thank you for putting up with my scatterbrained inattention and the scarcity of home-cooked meals. I love you all to pieces.

To Julia, thank you for working around my crazy schedule and delivering the corrected manuscripts in record time. You're awesome. To Jenna, Jean, and

Nancy, I don't know how you gals do that, but thank you for proofreading practically overnight. And to my sisters-in-law, thank you for reading every book and hounding me for the next one.

Lastly, to Charles, thank you for bringing the stories to life with your incredible narrations.

XOXO
I. T. Lucas

Made in the USA
Middletown, DE
30 October 2018